MW00412339

A Twist of Fate

A Novel

Tracye D. Bryant

Also, by
Tracye D. Bryant

This Twisted Life

A Lourdea! So much!
Thank you for your support! It was
such a welcome surprise
Pleas, you do hope you enjoy
the series and that each to you
character brings a smile to you
face.

Always,
Tracye Bryant

ISBN 978-0-9976946-4-2
Ebook ISBN 978-0-9976946-5-9

Printed in the United States of America

Cover Design
T. Bryant Media Group, Inc.

Cover Photography
Prime Phocus

For my boys, Avery, and Mason

Epigraph

Ecclesiastes 3:1 - *To everything there is a season, and a time to every purpose under the heaven....*

A Twist of Fate

Chapter 1

Alana woke up with the sun beaming through the cracks in the shades of the hotel room.

As she sat silently on the side of the bed, she felt an instant wave of shame at the thought of what took place the night before.

How could she give in so soon and so intently?

Although her guilt was no more than the fact that she had never done anything like this before, she knew it felt good. Her thoughts were startled by the sound of the toilet flushing in the bathroom. She quickly reached to put on her T-shirt that was on the floor beside the bed. She ran her fingers through her hair and could only imagine what she looked like.

"Good morning, beautiful," Rico said.

"Um, good morning," she replied softly.

"Did you sleep well?" he asked.

"Yeah, very well," she replied as she tiptoed past him to the restroom.

Alana closed the door as she entered the bathroom and smiled at herself in the mirror admiring her after-sex glow.

She and Rico had been seeing each other since the beginning of her second semester at NYU.
Her thoughts drifted back to the day she met him in the library. She wasn't paying attention to where she was walking and

accidently bumped into him causing him to spill his coffee all over his shirt.

"Oh my gosh! I am so sorry! Are you alright?" Alana gasped at the tall handsome man standing before her.

"Um, yeah. Perhaps you should be more careful when you are walking and pay attention," he said with a hint of aggravation in his voice.

Embarrassed, she looked inside her bag for tissues or napkins to help him clean up.

"I really am sorry. Listen, wait right here. Don't move!" she insisted as she turned in the direction of the nearest restroom.

She quickly returned with a handful of damp paper towels in a feeble attempt to clean up the mess she had caused. As she rounded the corner, she could see that the man was sitting at the table and had taken off his blue dress shirt, revealing a white wife-beater T-shirt, extremely toned muscles and an interesting tattoo of the Bible uniquely drawn inside a heart on his shoulder.

"Here, let me help you with that," she said as she grabbed the shirt off the back of the chair.

"Don't worry about it. I will have to take it to the dry cleaners to get the stain out. Luckily, I am done with class for today," he said with a much more pleasant smile.

Smiling, Alana was a bit relieved. She really did need to pay more attention to where she was going. Her friends teased her constantly about texting and walking.

"Well, sorry again," she said as she gathered her things to head for the door.

"Seeing as how you have scalded me with hot coffee, I, at least, deserve the pleasure of knowing your name," he smiled.

"Umm, Alana. Alana Coleman."

"Nice to meet you Miss Coleman," he said, extending his hand to shake hers.

"Rico. Rico Harris."

Alana's thoughts were interrupted by a light tap on the door. Caught up in her daydream, she'd forgotten for a minute where she was.

"Hey, you OK in there?"

"Ahhh, yeah. Sorry, on the way out now," she called out.

With a deep sigh, Alana quickly splashed water on her face and swished some mouthwash in her mouth. She smiled at herself in the mirror and headed back into the bedroom. Startled by all the lights on, she was even more surprised to find Rico fully dressed.

"Hey? Dressed so soon? I thought we were going to spend the day together?" she asked one question after the other.

"Ahh - yeah, sweetie, about that, I am going to have to take a rain check.

I just remembered I agreed to meet with some of my graduate students to discuss an upcoming assignment that they need some extra help with. Don't worry I will make it up to you," he said as he kissed the side of her cheek.

Frustrated with the response, Alana didn't bother looking at Rico. She angrily gathered her things from the floor and slid into her jeans and shirt. Trying feverishly not to appear upset, she searched for her shoes and her phone.

"OK, well – I guess, I will see you later then," she said with aggravation in her voice.

Alana did a quick last glance at the room to ensure that she hadn't forgotten anything and stormed out the door. With tears running down her face, she vowed never to be in that situation again with Rico. Ever since they had been seeing each other it seemed as though the only thing they did together was have sex. Rico seemed to always have something to do or somewhere to go and it was really pissing her off. As she made her way toward the subway station, she decided to give Bella a call.

"Hello," Bella answered half-asleep in a whisper.

"Belle, you up?"

"I am now. Alana, girl, why you calling so early? You sound like you're breathing hard. Is everything OK?"

"Yeah, I just need to talk. Can I come by?"

Glancing at the clock, Bella was really confused as to why Alana was even out at 8 o'clock on a Saturday morning, let alone trying to come by.

"Ummm, yeah. Sure," she said half-convincingly.

Before Bella could finish her sentence, the phone hung up and Alana was on the subway headed to her apartment. Looking at the clock again, Bella knew she only had about a half-hour before Alana arrived. She rolled over and gently planted soft kisses on Hustle's neck.

"Hey you. It's time to get up."

Rolling over, Hustle looked up into Bella's loving green eyes and pulled her head in to kiss her. Bella was smitten with Hustle and knew that her friends would never approve of their relationship or understand it.

"Why we getting up so early? I was thinking we could have breakfast in bed," said Hustle with a sly smile.

"My friend Alana is on her way here. She is in some sort of trouble, and I don't want to have to answer any unexpected questions about us once she gets here," Bella said as she stood and slipped on her flip flops.

"Well, when do you plan on telling them about me? Why are you ashamed of me? Of us?" Hustle asked with frustration.

Sucking her teeth and rolling her eyes, Bella turned to face her lover.

"No. No, I am not ashamed of you. And no, I am not ashamed of us, it's just that," Bella trailed off as she sat on the side of the bed with a long sigh and started rubbing her forehead.

"It's just what, BELLA?" Hustle said yelling.

"I don't understand why is it that I have been to New York to visit you at least a dozen times over the past two years and not once have I been able to meet your friends. It's like when you left California, you wanted to leave behind the life you came from and start all over again. I hear all these stories about you and Alana and Nehemiah and all the shit you all do at school and yet, they have no fucking clue that I even exist! Wait? They don't know do they?" Hustle asked standing over Bella and yelling.

"Hustle!" Bella yelled loudly.

Getting close up in Bella's face, Hustle didn't back down and started to yell back.
"No! Say it!" She said through clinched teeth.

"They don't know, do they Bella? Oh My Gosh! That's it! They do not know that little miss goodie-two-shoes Bella is a fucking lesbian!" Hustle screamed at the top of her lungs, twirling around in the middle of the floor tossing her hands in the air.

"Look, I'm sorry. Ok? I'm just not ready to tell them that I'm in a gay relationship," Bella said softly. "The past two years I've worked hard to have a normal life with people who love me for me, and I don't want to mess that up!"

"Love you for you? Are you kidding me? They don't even know you, so who exactly do they love, Bella?" Seems to me like you are trying to be something you're not for the sake of what other people may think," Hustle said loudly and furiously.

"Hustle, it's not like that and you know it!"

"Yeah? Well, it sure as hell looks like it," she said as she headed down the hall to the bathroom.

Bella looked up from the side of the bed fighting back tears in her eyes. She loved Hustle and knew that this was the one thing that continued to jeopardize their relationship. Her inability to cope with what people would think about her being a lesbian had taken its toll on her emotionally for years. It was true, she chose to come to New York for school in hopes that she could start a new life and somehow be different. But she couldn't help herself, she was just attracted to women, and she really loved Hustle.

Chapter 2

"Damn it! I swear I need a new car," Josh said frustrated at the black smoke billowing out of his 2004 Ford Explorer. Pulling over on I-285, Josh put the truck in park and searched the back seat for a bottle of motor oil. Realizing the one he had was empty, he sighed heavily and called his dad.

"Son," Tyrone answered looking at the early morning time on the clock. "Shouldn't you be at work?"

"Dad, my truck is running hot again, and I am on the side of the freeway on 285! Can you come pick me up?" Not realizing his tone or elevation in his voice, Josh was pissed at the thought of the truck and being late for work.

"Josh, did you put oil in the truck like I told you last week?" Tyrone scolded.

Rolling his eyes, Josh exclaimed: "Dad! I have been putting oil in here week after week for the past few months, I told you and Mom, I need a new car!"

"Hold on, boy. Who you yelling at?"

"Sorry," he said with a deep sigh. "Look, Dad, I really need you to come get me if you can, please."

"Where are you, Josh?"

"I am just past the Washington Road exit on 285 going toward Cascade."

"Alright, I'm on my way."

As he hung up the phone, Tyrone understood the frustration his son was experiencing.

However, he was trying to dissuade him from getting a new car with graduation just around the corner. He and Josh's mom, Sherita, had already decided to buy him a new car as a graduation gift and needed to keep it a secret for at least a couple more months.

Smiling at the thought of the look on his son's face when that day comes, Tyrone quickly glanced at a stack of new car brochures on his nightstand. He'd been researching and doing price comparisons for months. Josh was gonna love it.

"Hello? Umm, yeah, may I speak with the manager-on-duty, please?" Josh tried desperately not to sound so agitated.

"Hold on," the voice on the other end said without enthusiasm.

"Thank you for calling Foot Locker at Greenbriar Mall. This is Sheryl. How may I help you?"

"Hey Ms. Sheryl. This is Josh. How are you?"

"I'm fine Josh. Where you at?" She said with a slight attitude in her voice.

"Umm, my truck ran hot, and I am on 285 by Washington Road waiting on my dad to pick me up shortly. I should be there within the hour. Is that OK?"

"Umhmm, you know we already short-staffed today and this is one of the busiest weekends with these new Jordans that was released today. You might as well consider this your lunch break. Aight then, see you whenever you get here," Sheryl said with sarcasm. "Thank you. I will be there short…," before he could finish his sentence, she'd hung up the phone.

Mad and aggravated, Josh couldn't wait until the year was over and he would be off to college and not worried about the job, the truck, nothing! As he shook his head, he looked at the clock. It was 9:40 a.m., Tracy should be up by now.

"Hello," Tracy answered with a dry tone.

"Hey. Good morning. Everything OK?" Josh asked, a bit taken aback at his girlfriend's lack of excitement to hear his voice.

"Why aren't you at work?" she quizzed.

Sighing, he says "my truck broke down on 285 and I am waiting on my dad to come get me. What's wrong with you this morning?"

Knowing she needed to change her tone, Tracy tried to sound more concerned at Josh being on the side of the road.

"Oh, no! Are you OK?" she asked with forced concern.

"Yeah. I told you, my dad is on the way. Listen, if you were busy or something, I can talk to you later when I get off work."

"Alright. Call me later," she said with an attitude and hung up.

Lying back on the bed, Tracy knew she wasn't going to be able to keep this up much longer with Josh. She had to somehow tell him she was 6 weeks pregnant, and she wasn't sure if it was even his. She'd reconnected a few weeks ago with her old boyfriend Jude at a party and had a little too much to drink. One thing led to another and the next thing she knew she and Jude were in a back bedroom. It all happened so quickly she didn't know what to do afterward. And now, more than five over the counter pregnancy tests confirm positive, she has to tell Josh and her parents.

Tracy suddenly felt nauseous as she rubbed her hands across her stomach at the thought of a baby. What was she going to do? She could barely afford to take care of herself. How was this going to work?

Tyrone pulled up behind the still-smoking truck and couldn't help but grin at his son's visible frustration. Josh quickly gathered all of his things from the truck and locked the doors.
"Son, you look like you need a ride," Tyrone said jokingly.

"Don't start Dad. I am really not in the mood," Josh said as he got in the car. This day was already not starting out good and to think it was only 10 o'clock.

A Twist of Fate

Chapter 3

The sounds of birds chirping in the distance, the light morning breeze sneaking through the cracked window, the mixed aroma of exotic flowers and breakfast cooking brought a smile to Sherita's face.

It was always a pleasant surprise waking up in her little paradise in Trinidad. Ever since she and Kroy got married, for the first few months she would pinch herself throughout the day to make sure she wasn't dreaming. The past two years have certainly been a whirlwind and she finally feels as though this is the life she was meant to live.

As she turned on her side and lingered a bit more gazing at the sun through the window, she heard a light tap at the door.

"Good morning, Mi' Amore," Kroy said smiling as he entered the room with a tray of fresh berries, a small vase of Martinique Wild Purple Orchids and a small glass of orange juice.

"Hmmm, good morning, honey. Looks like you've been busy," Sherita said lovingly as she sat up in bed and awaited the gift before her.

"Yeah, I guess you could say I got an early start to the day. I wanted to make sure you had a nice breakfast before we head for the airport to go back to the States."

Sucking her teeth and posing a pretend frown on her face.

"Ahhh.... Do we have to go already? Please, sweetie – just one more day?" she pleaded.

"Mi' Amore, we've been here for two weeks already, a week longer than we intended to stay, don't you think we should get back and check on things in Atlanta?" Kroy said with his thick Caribbean accent.

"Besides, we can use this as motivation to move forward with our plans to bring the family over to Trinidad for spring break in a few months. You can come to Trinidad anytime you want.

Mummy and them love having you here and if they had their way, we would never leave!" he said smiling.

"I know, I know. I guess you're right. I do miss Josh and Kendra. I just wish it wasn't so expensive to call them or else I would truly reach out and touch them by phone," she said with a chuckle.

Smiling adoringly at his wife, Kroy sat along the side of the bed as she started to eat her breakfast. It was his pleasure to see her smile and be happy. As they approached their 2-year wedding anniversary, their life together had started out somewhat rocky.

Sherita's kids weren't that thrilled about their mom getting married and especially so soon after having lost her lover Lamont. Kroy and Josh have managed to establish a small relationship with one another, but Kroy knew that deep down Josh still wasn't happy with the arrangement. It had been an adjustment for everyone. Kroy was getting used to living in Atlanta and trying diligently to maintain his family import business overseas. Sherita didn't seem to mind, she enjoyed the travel and especially loved visiting the in-laws in Trinidad and just being on the beach.

"Mi' Amore! Mon Amour let's go! We are going to miss the cab!" Kroy yelled in the house for his wife to hurry with her goodbyes.

"Oh, keep your shirt on son she's coming!" yelled Auhnna, Kroy's mother as she hugged Sherita one last time.

"Go now, before we have to come up with an excuse to keep you here yet another week, gurl," she said with a smile.

"Oh, thank you for everything, Mummy. I appreciate you guys so much. I promise we will be back soon." Sherita, grabbed her purse and gave a last hug and kiss to her father-in-law and brother-in-law and headed out the door.

Kroy was standing anxiously outside the cab with the door held open looking at his watch.

Auhnna came out and gave her son a quick kiss on the cheek and they were off. It was always sad leaving the Port of Spain, the weather, the food, the music, the beach – everything Sherita could have ever dreamed of. She really needed to get Josh and Alana here next year, she thought.

"Maybe we should consider buying a vacation home here," she thought to herself.

But she still hadn't decided what to do with the $150,000 cash that Allison left her. It's been invested for the past two years and has earned quite a bit of profit thus far. Maybe she will discuss it with Josh and Alana and see how they feel about the idea, they've been a little wishy washy lately when it comes to this new life.

"Penny for your thoughts," Kroy interrupted as he grabbed Sherita's hand.

"Huh? Oh, nothing sweetie, just thinking about the kids that's all. I need to call them when we get to Miami."

"That would be good."

There is always such a line going through customs in Trinidad, it is the one part of the trip that Sherita and Kroy both could do without. Once they finally boarded the plane, they settled in for their two-and-a half-hour flight to Miami. As she reached for her seat belt, Sherita felt a sharp pain run down the side of her abdomen.

"Umph," she said wincing.

"You OK, sweetie?" Kroy asked with a look of concern on his face.

"Umm, yeah, just a sharp pain in my side, but I'm good, baby. It's nothing," she replied.

"Love, that is the second time in I know 3 months you've complained about that pain. Why won't you just go to the doctor and get it checked? Just to be on the safe side. Please?"

Putting her hand on her husband's leg for reassurance she says: "Yes, honey. I promise. I will call next week when we get back."

The soft voice over the loudspeaker gave instructions on the safety precautions of the flight.

As the plane taxied slowly down the runway, Sherita gazed out the small window with a hint of concern on her face. Kroy was right, she had felt the sting of the pain a few months ago and several times since then. She hadn't bothered to tell anyone since she did not want to raise concern. The pain grew more and more intense each time. She would call and schedule an appointment with her primary care doctor first thing Monday morning.

Lord I am trusting in you, she prayed.

Chapter 4

Kendra paced the floor back and forth with the phone in her hand contemplating on calling Rico.
She hadn't heard from him since Tuesday and was a bit worried. It wasn't like him to go this long without calling her at least to say hello.

"God what was I thinking? This long-distance relationship shit is not working for me," she said to herself.

Kendra met Rico 6 months ago in June at her cousin Harold's funeral in Virginia. She spent a few days in the city with family, and Rico was close friends with one of her cousins. He had come to pay his respects from New York and was hella fine.

"Shit!" she sighed as she sat on the chair in her room by the window. Just as she gazed out over the yard and her thoughts began to wander, the phone rang. She answered immediately.

"Hello."

"Hey, you, how's it going?"

It was him.

"Hmph, how's it goin?" Kendra said with an attitude. "Rico it's been 3 days since I last spoke with you! Where da'hell you been?"

"Hey, hey, calm down. I'm sorry, sweetie, I've just been busy with work and stuff. Nothing to be mad about," he tried to explain.

"Listen, we've been through this time and time again and I told you, I am already not fond of this long-distance love shit and because I want more than what I am getting I think we should just not do this anymore."

"Wait a minute. You are jumping to conclusions here. It is the first time in the 6 months that we've known each other that I haven't called every day on a consistent basis; and I miss 1, maybe 2, days and already you want to break up with me? Come on Kendra, we have got to work through this – I just think you are flying off the handle for no reason. I told you, I've just been busy with work. The semester is ending, I have lots of exams to conduct, papers to grade and students who wait until the last minute to get their shit together. That is all! Nothing more. Now, can we start over? Please?" he said pleading.

Kendra sat anxiously listening on the side of the bed with her foot twitching away. She knew she really shouldn't be mad. After all, what else could the man do? Hell, he's on the phone now and she certainly didn't want to waste an early morning phone call with an argument.

"I'm sorry," she conceded with a sigh. "I know I shouldn't automatically assume the worst, but this is all very new to me, and I am still trying to decide if the adventure of a long-distance love is what I want right now."

"Ahh, baby, I know. It is tough to get used to. But hey, I think we are doing fine. Besides, you are still coming here to New York in a couple of weeks for the weekend, right?"

"Huh? Oh, yeah – that is my plan. You still want me to come?" she asked with hesitation.

"Yes, baby of course I do. I can't wait to spend some more time with you and just make you smile. And besides there is nothing in the world like Times Square and New York City!"

"I'd like that. Hell, I need that," she said with a chuckle.

"So, now that we've gotten all that past us, how have you been pretty lady?"

"Well, I am OK – I think. I have been battling an upset stomach for a few days, but otherwise, I guess I am OK."

"Sounds like somebody is a little lovesick, huh? I do wish I could've stayed longer than a couple of days last month, but you know…duty calls," Rico chimed.

"Yeah, I know. I am really hoping that you will plan to come back to Atlanta at the end of January for my birthday celebration. I am planning on throwing a nice party with all my friends and, besides, I really want you to meet my best friend Sherita."

"You got it! Just text me the dates in the next day or so and I will start looking at the flights and planning accordingly. Hey, maybe after the party we can sneak away to one of those cabins in the mountains, don't they have those in Georgia?" he asked dreamingly.

Laughing, Kendra replied "ah, yes, there are cabins in Georgia, silly. However, I don't know that we will have time to do all of that in a weekend, but we will look into it."

"Cool. OK– sweetie, I am about to hop on the subway and head home. I will holla at you a little later, OK?"

"OK. Get home safe. Miss you much."

"I will. Bye."

Kendra hung up the phone and smiled, she really felt a connection to this man who she barely knew. She loved how he is so down to earth and educated with just the right hint of "thug" in him. Who knew she would meet someone who seemed so perfect at a funeral?

As she looked at the clock, she realized Sherita was coming home today. She missed her and although she loved Kroy to death, she was still getting use to him whisking her friend away on trips for weeks at a time. Kendra was happy for Sherita. She had been through so much the past 2 years, she deserved to be happy. Hell, her kids were grown, and she didn't have money to worry about with that huge inheritance Allison left her. She was entitled to live this dream of a life.

Kendra headed toward the bathroom to start the shower and all of a sudden, she felt nauseated. She ran and barely made it in before she was throwing up in the toilet.

After a few minutes of endless vomiting, she was able to gain her composure enough to sit on the side of the tub. Rubbing her stomach, she searched her brain for everything she had eaten over the past couple of days. Something truly didn't agree with her stomach and for the past week she has just been all out of sorts.

She decided to take a quick shower and then lay back down for a while to see if the feeling would subside.

Kendra woke up startled at the sound of the phone ringing. She hazily glanced at the clock. Shit! It was 2:50 she must've fallen back asleep. "What is wrong with me," she thought to herself as she answered the blaring phone.

"Hello!" she said yelling and rushing.

"Kendra girl, are you still at home?" Sherita said with a hint of annoyance in her voice.

"Um, yeah, I'm sorry Sher, I thought I was just lying back down for a minute earlier and must've dozed back asleep. Are you guys at the airport? I am on my way!" she said with a ramble.

"Kendra! Kendra! Girl, never mind – we took a taxi, it's no problem. And besides, it would take you at least 20 or 30 minutes to get here anyway, by then we will be at home. No worries. Just give me a call later this afternoon when you get it together," Sherita said with a playful tone and chuckle.

"Yeah, alright. Sher, I really am sorry. I was looking forward to picking you guys up at the airport and seeing you today."

"Well, you can still come see me Kendra, I am only going to Southwest Atlanta!" she said sarcastically.

"Ha ha, very funny, heffa," Kendra responded while rolling her eyes at her friend's dry sense of humor.

"OK, well let me get up and get going and I will be at your house in an hour or so. Is that cool? Or do you and lover boy need some "alone" time?"

"Girl, look – me and "lover boy" would've done that plus some by the time your slow ass get here, so just you worry about finding your way and bringing a nice bottle of Chardonnay to get us through the night," Sherita laughed.

"Bye girl. See you in a bit."

"OK Kendra."

Sherita missed Kendra, she loved traveling, but she loved her girlfriend time as well. She couldn't wait to just kick back and catch up. She and Kendra hadn't spent any real time together in a few months. Being married comes with a whole new life for Sherita. And since Kendra has been all hot and heavy with this new guy she met, the two have been hanging on through phone conversations.

A Twist of Fate

Chapter 5

Alana heard loud shouting voices as she made it to Bella's apartment. Bella didn't indicate that she had company, she hoped that everything was alright. She banged on the door anxiously, not sure what to expect on the other side.

"BELLA! It's me Alana, open up!" she yelled through the door.

There was an abrupt silence as the voices drew to a hush tone and the only thing that Alana could hear was movement inside the apartment. After what seemed like eons, Bella finally opened the door.

"Hey, Alana. Sorry it took so long, come on in," Bella said with a forced cheerful tone and smile.

Alana could tell Bella had been crying.

"Ah, Bella – is everything alright?"

"Girl, yeah, everything is fine. I am good. Everything is OK, I promise."

"Bella, I heard loud shouting from your apartment as I made it to the top of the stairs. Who were you fighting with?" Alana asked, not convinced of the front her friend was putting on.

Before Bella could answer the question, Hustle emerged from the bedroom, fully dressed.

"Yeah – Bella, who were you 'fighting' with?" Hustle asked in a sarcastic manner, glaring angrily at her lover sitting across the room.

"Hello," Alana said surprised as she looked Hustle up and down.

As Hustle walked across the room, she politely introduced herself to Alana.

"Hey, what's up? I'm Hustle."

"Nice to meet you, I am Alana."

"Bella, I'm sorry – girl if I had known you had company, I would have waited until later this afternoon to come by…. I certainly didn't mean to interrupt…"

"No, no – we are glad you came by Alana. Bella has told me so much about you and this is as good a time as any to meet you. Isn't it Bella?" Hustle asked with insistence.

The tension in the room was thick enough to cut with a knife. As Bella and Hustle glared back and forth at one another, Alana couldn't help but feel a bit uncomfortable, as if she had just opened Pandora's Box.

"Alana, this is my girlfriend Hustle from Cali, she and I are…" Bella felt a large lump in her throat as she wasn't sure what to say to Alana. How would she take the news of her being a lesbian?

"We are what Bella?" Hustle was angry.

"She and I are……uhm."

Bella felt flush in the face. This was the first time in years she had to publicly announce her sexuality to anyone.

She had worked so hard to keep that life a secret, and it kept resurfacing, forcing her to face the realities of the situation.

"Bella. Girl, you're scaring me. What is going on?" Alana asked as she sat on the edge of the sofa with a concerned look on her face.

"Alana, Hustle and I are lovers," Bella had streams of tears coming down her face as she covered her eyes with her hands and sobbed lightly.

Hustle stood in shock and relieved that Bella made the announcement. However, she couldn't help but feel sad for her girlfriend. It was never her intention to hurt Bella.

"Wait? Did you just say lovers? As in lovers, lovers? Like lesbian lovers?" Alana said spewing one question after the other.

"When the hell did this happen? Why have you never said anything about being…. being gay?" Alana wasn't sure how to get the words out. She wasn't quite sure how to respond. It really didn't matter to her that Bella was a lesbian; she still loved her and appreciated their friendship. It was obvious that this was a painful part of her life that she struggled with acknowledging.

"Lan, I've been a lesbian since middle school. Hustle and I have been together since my junior year in high school, and we've been through hell and back regarding our relationship. We could never get approval from our families about our lifestyle and just in an effort to keep the peace, we just basically kept it to ourselves. Well, I guess, I am the one that has been keeping it a secret," she explained.

Stunned and unsure of what to say, Alana felt a sense of sorrow for her friend. She and Bella had been friends since the first day they met freshman year at the financial aid office, and although she never really seen her express any interest in guys, she didn't think anything of it. Bella and Nehemiah had become like siblings to Alana and all she knew is that it really didn't matter to her if Bella liked women; she just wanted to figure out how she could help her through this trying and disturbing time.

"OK, OK – listen, now everything will be alright," Alana said. "Let's just figure this whole thing out. What is the problem with you all being open and in love now? I mean, I don't care that the two of you are…. you know, whatever, that's your business."

"Wow – look at 'little Miss Holier Than Thou' in the room this morning," Hustle shouted. "You really think it's that simple for us? Huh? You think just because you've decided that in your eyes we are 'all good' that it makes it alright? Well, let me tell you something, I have lost everything because of this relationship! Everything! My family has disowned me, I've done things that are so out of my character just to help keep BELLA's ass in school – to help her keep this fucking secret! So, no, we don't need your approval or pity!"

Alana was dumbfounded. Here she thought she was attempting to be supportive of this strange and secret relationship and it somehow appeared as though she was being attacked. She walked slowly toward Hustle, looking her square in the eye.

"Look here, Hustle or whatever the hell your name is, to be honest with you, I could give a damn what you've been through or

experienced to live this 'lifestyle' as you put it. I honestly don't
care if you pack your shit and head for the

nearest bus station and never come back. My only concern and
sympathy is for Bella. She is my friend, gay or not and I am
certain that however long it takes her to get through it or get over it
she will do just that, and I plan to be there every step of the way.
So, just because your life hasn't turned out the way you wanted
cause yo' ass decided to chase rainbows in the sky, that's on you!"
Alana was mad.

Just as Hustle was about to make an abrupt move toward Alana,
Bella stepped in between the two.

"Whoa! Hold on you two. Listen, this is getting a little out of
hand. Listen Lan, thank you – I couldn't have asked for a better
friend, but this is something Hustle and I must work through on
our own. Hustle, please leave the room for a minute?"

Hustle rolled her eyes at Alana as she headed back into the
bedroom. In her heart, she knew that this friendship with Alana
needed to end and end soon. She may be an unwanted influence on
Bella, and she'd worked too hard to keep their somewhat rocky
relationship intact, and the last thing she needed was someone like
Alana changing her mind.

"Lan, I am so sorry that I didn't tell you. I, I just don't know what
to say," Bella said embarrassed as she sat down on the couch.

Alana kneeled down beside the chair next to Bella and placed her
hand on her knee.

"Bella, I really meant what I said about not caring that you're a
lesbian. Nothing about that lifestyle changes how I feel about you

42

or our friendship. You are truly one of the smartest people I know and extremely creative and I truly believe that once you are completely comfortable with who you are and how you are, you'll be able to live freely with whomever you choose to do so. Even if it is that "Hustle headache."

Smiling at her friend's acceptance, Bella chuckled lightly at the fact that Alana didn't seem to care much for Hustle. She really could be a dramatic handful at times.

"Thanks Lan. I appreciate it."

"Hey, so enough about me, what is going on with you? Why are you here so early in the morning trying to help me work out my unusual life?" Bella asked with curiosity.

Sitting completely Indian style on the floor at this point, Alana felt a sense of shame as she looked at her friend.

"Alana, girl, what is it? Is it Rico?" Bella asked with concern.

"Bella, I think I'm pregnant."

Bella's eyes got as wide as half-dollar coins as she stifled her gasp by putting her hand over her mouth.

"Pregnant!?"

"Are you sure? How do you know? I mean what happened? Wait! Isn't he still…married, Alana?"

Bella's questions were coming one after the other and Alana wasn't able to get a word in edgewise to make sense of it all.

"Bella, girl, no I'm not sure, I just know I've missed my last two cycles and I feel all weird throughout the day. I am not sure what is going on with him and his wife, because he never talks about it. However, the only thing we do together is screw and it is really pissing me off. I feel like he's not being honest with me, and I just don't know what to do."

"Well Lan, have you told him?"

"No, I haven't said anything to anyone but you, just now."

"You have to tell him. He has to take responsibility for this. Girl, you know how I have felt about him since day one – hmph, fraternizing with the students and all."

"Belle, it wasn't like that. We are both adults and I knew exactly what I was getting into."

"Girl, that is some bullshit! What the hell are you gonna do with a baby? In New York? By a married professor?" Bella was furious.

Alana sat silently on the floor with tears in her eyes. She hadn't thought about any of that, all she could think about was her mom and dad. How would she tell them and destroy their dreams for her? She knew she needed to tell Rico, but she also needed to be sure.

"Bella, please promise me you won't say anything about this to anyone. Promise me!"

Taking a deep breath and realizing the scared and frustrated look in her friend's eyes, Bella agreed to keep her secret.

"OK, Lan, I got your back. But you have got to go to the infirmary to get confirmation on this and then we need to figure out what to do next," Bella said as she stood to hug her friend.

As the two stood in the living room in a loving embrace, Hustle stood silently in the doorway of the bedroom listening to the conversation.

"Well, what do you know, little Miss Goodie-Two-Shoes is knocked up by a married professor. I wonder what type of support she'd get if that information got out?" Hustle thought to herself with a look of deceit on her face.

Chapter 6

"Josh! Josh! – man wake up! Your break is over. You need to get back out on the floor before Ms. Shirley come back here and find you asleep!" said Roderick, his shoe store co-worker.

"Huh? Oh, yeah – thanks man. Let me run to the restroom and I will be right out."

Josh was exhausted. He'd been working nonstop over the past week to try and get as many hours as possible to save up for a car. His truck was still on the fritz and luckily his stepdad Kroy was nice enough to give him a lift to and from work. But he was feeling the effects of the 12- and 15-hour days. He needed a day off just to sleep.

"Josh, boy where you been? You shoulda been back from break 15 minutes ago!" Ms. Shirley chastised.

"I know. I'm sorry. I am not really feeling that well, would it be alright if I go home?"

"Hmph, I guess that will be fine. We are slow right now anyway. Go ahead and go," she said with strained compassion.

Josh clocked out and grabbed his book bag out of the locker. As he headed out the door, he realized he didn't have a car. He was going to have to find a ride or catch the bus. He certainly wasn't in the mood for that today. He called Sherita.

"Come on Ma, answer the phone," he said to himself as it continued to ring and ring before her voicemail came on.

Looking at his watch, he wondered where she could be at 11 a.m. on a Wednesday? Normally, she would be at home.

He hung up and called Kroy. As the phone rang and rang, Josh was becoming annoyed. Why wasn't anybody answering the phone? As far as he knew, Tyrone and Felicia were out of town, so he couldn't call his dad.

"Hello?"

"Hey Tracy, it's me. How are you?" he asked delicately.

Tracy had been a bit distant the past week or so. Josh just wasn't sure what was going on with her and tried to just give her some space.

"I'm fine. Why aren't you at work?"

"That's why I am calling. Would you be able to come give me a ride home? I am leaving early. I am just tired and exhausted from working so much and decided to go home."

"Um, yeah, it will be about 30 minutes or so before I get there, I am coming from downtown," she said casually.

"OK. Let me know when you get here, I will be out in front of Macy's."

As Tracy hung up, the nurse came in the room to hand her a prescription for prenatal vitamins. At 6-and-a-half weeks pregnant, it was time she started preparing for what's to come.

As she left the doctor's office, she saw Sherita and Kroy in the waiting room.

"Shit!" she said to herself.

"Tracy! Hi honey, how are you?" Sherita said with a smile and surprised to see her.

"Um, Mrs. Coleman – I mean, Mrs. LeBeauf, how are you?"

"I am well, honey, how are you? I didn't know that Dr. Snieder was your doctor?" Sherita said with concern.

"Yes ma'am, he is. I had to come for a check-up."

"I see. Well, I trust that all is well. It is good to see you, Tracy. Take care."

Sherita and Kroy waited patiently to be seen by the doctor. Sherita continued to experience the excruciating abdominal pains more frequently since they had returned home from Trinidad.

"Sherita Coleman?" the nurse called from the door.

"Yes, that's me. My new last name is LeBeauf. I'm sorry I haven't changed that information in your records."

"No problem, Mrs. LeBeauf, my apologies. Right this way."

Sherita and Kroy made their way to the small white room in the back. Nervous and scared, Sherita proceeded to undress as instructed and waited to be examined by the doctor.

"Hey Tracy – you here?" Josh said as he answered the phone.

"Yeah, I'm out front."

Joshed sensed there was something wrong when he got in the car. He and Tracy had been arguing over the dumbest stuff lately. He certainly didn't want to upset her, and he wasn't in the mood for a fight.

Leaning over to kiss her, he asked, "how you doin?"

"I'm good," she said coyly as she gave him her cheek.

"Hey, what's going on with us? I feel like we have done nothing but fight over the past few weeks and I'm not sure what I did to make you so upset," Josh said.

Taking a deep breath, Tracy knew she couldn't hold it any longer. She needed to tell Josh about the baby. Tracy was somewhat fidgety as they sat at the red light leaving the mall.

"Josh, I need to tell you something."

"OK."

"Um, I don't want you to be upset with me and please know that I love you more than anything."

"OK. What's going on? You're making me nervous," he said with a look of concern on his face.

"Josh."

Josh was feeling a bit intense. He had never seen Tracy so at a loss for words. The past month had been weird with her, flying off the handle at the least little thing and not really wanting to hang out, he just assumed that their relationship was turning a tide. Just as

Tracy pressed the gas to turn on the arrow signal, everything went blank. All of a sudden it seemed as though the two were in a never-ending roller coaster. The last thing Josh remembered was Tracy's shrieking screams and then there was nothing.

"Sir! Sir! Can you hear me?" yelled a strange voice.

Josh was disoriented and felt a horrible pain in his head.

"Sir! Do you know where you are? Sir? Can you hear me?"

"Umm…Tracy? Where is Trac…" Josh was fading in and out.

"Sir, my name is Adam. You were in a car accident. Sir, you are going to be alright. Can you tell me your name?"

Josh, finally able to compose himself, glanced up as he listened to the paramedic.

"Umm…Josh. My name is Joshua Coleman. What's going on? Where's my girlfriend?"

"Sir, everything is going to be alright. We are going to transport you to Piedmont Hospital and get you all checked out."

The paramedics loaded Josh onto a stretcher and into the back of an ambulance. From the distance, he could see the mangled remains of two or three cars, including the one that he and Tracy were riding in. But he still didn't see his girlfriend.

"Sir, I am Elicia, and I am the EMT that will take care of you until we get to the hospital. Are you OK to answer a few questions?"

"Yeah, but please, please tell me where is my girlfriend, Tracy? Is she OK?" Josh asked with a look of grave concern on his face.

"Sir, your girlfriend is on the way to Piedmont as well. She is in another ambulance. Let me get some information from you and make sure you are OK. Can you tell me your full name?"

"Joshua Malik Coleman."

"Ok, great – Joshua, do you know your birthday?

"Umm, June 11, 1994."

"Do you know what day it is?"

"Umm, Wednesday. Hey, listen, I am fine, where is my girlfriend? And what about my phone? I need to call my mom and my dad," Josh was getting irritated.

"Ok, sir, I understand. But I do need you to remain calm. Your girlfriend is headed to the hospital as well. One of my colleagues is taking good care of her in the other vehicle. Now please answer just a few more questions and we will be at the hospital soon."

"Yeah, OK."

"It looks as though you took a nasty blow to the forehead. Luckily, the seatbelt locked securely in place and stopped you from going through the windshield. Also, because of the size of the car, it is really a good thing the airbag didn't deploy on contact or else you would be looking at facial injuries. Your blood pressure is stable, and your vital signs are normal.

Once we get to the ER, they will give you a thorough overview and determine whether you need to be admitted for observation."

"Sir, I believe this is your cellphone," indicated a man who stuck his head in from the front part of the vehicle.

"Yes. Thank you. Umm, can I call my mom?"

"Sure."

Josh's mind was going a mile-a-minute. What happened? Was Tracy OK? He needed to call his mom.

Sherita and Kroy were pulling up to lunch at the Feed Store in College Park when the phone started to ring.

"MOM! Mom!"

"Josh! Honey, is everything OK? What's wrong? What's all that noise in the background?" Sherita was nervous.

"Mom, I'm fine. Tracy and I were in an accident and I am headed to Piedmont Hospital…"
Before Josh could say more, Sherita accidentally hung up the phone and told Kroy to turn the car around.

"Oh my God! Josh is at Piedmont Hospital; he's been in an accident!" she yelled at Kroy as she tried to focus on her phone to call Tyrone.

"MOM!!!" Josh yelled realizing that the shock of the news made Sherita hang up.

"It's going to be OK, Mi' Amore', just calm down," Kroy insisted.

"DON'T TELL ME TO FUCKING CALM DOWN! DID YOU NOT HEAR ME? MY BABY WAS IN A CAR ACCIDENT AND I NEED TO GET TO HIM NOW! SO DON'T FUCKING TELL ME TO CALM DOWN, JUST GET THIS DAMN CAR THERE AS QUICKLY AS POSSIBLE!" Sherita was furious and scared.

"OK, OK… I hear you. But, sweetheart, you are going to need to calm down long enough to at least tell me what hospital we are going to?" Kroy was being very calm and understanding. He knew his wife was frightened.

"Umm… Piedmont. Piedmont Hospital on Peachtree Street," she said with a deep breath and massaging the temples on her head.

"Hello...this is MRS. Coleman speaking, how may I help you?" Felicia answered with an attitude. She still hadn't quite gotten over the fact that Sherita and Tyrone shared a special and unique bond.

"Yeah, Felicia, this is Sherita. May I speak with Tyrone, please?" Sherita completely discounted Felicia's curt tone and apparent attitude.

"I'm sorry, Sherita, Tyrone is taking a nap right now. Can I give him a message?"

"Look, Felicia – can you please wake him up? Josh has been in a car accident and was rushed to the hospital. I need to speak with him now," Sherita was trying to keep calm.

"Oh, no! Sorry to hear that...what hosp..."

"LOOK HEFFA! I ain't got time to hem and haw wit yo' crazy ass today! Now put Tyrone on the phone and stop with all this bullshit you got goin' on!"

Mad at being disrespected, Felicia had no other choice but to comply. She hurriedly went into the living room where Tyrone was napping on the couch. She nudged him intently and handed him the phone as she stormed out of the room.

"It's yo' ex!" she said with an attitude.

"Hello?"

"Ty, it's Sher – Josh was involved in a car accident, and he's been taken to Piedmont Hospital. Can you meet me there?" Sherita didn't waste any time getting to the point.

"Oh no, is he OK? Yeah, yeah… I'm on my way – I, I will be there in 10 minutes."

Tyrone was anxiously putting on his shoes and grabbing his keys and wallet off the table before heading out the door.

While Sherita focused on answering Tyrone's questions, she sighed trying to remain calm. She was nervous.

"I don't know. I am headed there now. He called, he sounded scared, but I don't know much more than that. I will see you shortly."

"Yeah OK."

The doors to the ambulance swung open and startled Josh.

As they were getting him out the vehicle, he could see a swarm of paramedics surrounding what appeared to be Tracy on the stretcher leading into the emergency room. They were all yelling and moving rapidly as they rushed to get her inside the building.

Josh heard one of them yell, "She's CRASHING!" as another jumped on top of the moving bed and began administering rapid chest compressions.

"TRACY!" he yelled helplessly as she disappeared through the sliding glass doors.

Chapter 7

"Ms. White, looks like congratulations are in order for you!"

"Huh? So, it's true? I'm … gonna have a baby?" Kendra was in shock.

"Yes, it is true. You are going to have a baby. And by the looks of it, I would say you are just shy of 12 weeks. We will have a more accurate due date once we get you in the office for an ultrasound. Unfortunately, on Saturdays we only do limited services in an effort to just give patients the option when they can't make their appointments during the week," Dr. Ashley Jae explained.

"Wow. OK. So, what do I do now?" Kendra was nervous. She always wanted kids growing up, but once she turned 40 and had never been married nor had children, she put that thought out of her mind.

"Well, the obvious, like be sure to eat three healthy and balanced meals per day. It is OK to snack throughout the day; I would just recommend healthy snack choices. Limited amounts of caffeine and no alcohol."

"Wait… No alcohol! Can I give that up next week? Hell, I need something to get through the shock of this shit," Kendra was serious.

"It is not recommended that you consume any alcohol while pregnant, Ms. White. I do understand being in shock. By the looks of it, this is totally not what you were expecting?"

"No, not at all. I was thinking… hell, I was praying it was the stomach flu; just my damn luck."

"Nope. Not the flu. But I think that once you wrap your mind around it, you will be excited. First-time pregnancies can be overwhelming, but I assure you, you are very healthy; and as long as you follow my instructions, eat right, moderately exercise and take your vitamins you will be fine," Dr. Jae was being extremely empathetic.

"Yeah. I am sure I will."

"Well, if there is nothing more, I will have the nurse bring you in a prescription for your prenatal vitamins and I will see you back in about four to six weeks. Congratulations again!"

Kendra was in a daze as she finished putting on her clothes. She didn't even notice when the nurse entered the room.

"Oh, hi Ms. White! Good to see you. Your friend Ms. Coleman, I mean Mrs. LaBeauf was just in here about an hour ago," the young nurse said cheerfully.

"Umm, good to see you, too. Thank you."

As Kendra searched her purse for her keys, her phone started buzzing. She'd put it on vibrate when she got to the doctor's office and didn't realize she had several missed calls from Sherita.

"Hello…"

"Kendra! Girl, where have you been? I have been calling you for two hours!" Sherita was frantic.

"Umm, sorry. I was at an appointment. Sher, what's wrong? Is everything OK?"

"No. Well, yes and no. Josh and Tracy were in a car accident earlier today. We are at Piedmont Hospital."

"Sher – is he OK? I am on my way there now! Just calm down and tell me what happened and what is going on?"

Kendra quizzed Sherita as she got in the car and headed down I-75 South.

"Girl, Josh is fine. He just has a few bumps and bruises and shook up, but praise be to God, he is OK. However, Tracy is in emergency surgery. She wasn't wearing a seatbelt and the impact of the collision really banged her up pretty bad. We are all here now waiting to see what is going on. They are going to keep Josh overnight for observation since he took such a blow to the head. We are waiting on a room now."

"Sher, it is all going to be alright. I am on the way there now. Hang in there. I am sure that Tracy will be fine and this will all be OK before you know it. Are her parents there?"

"Ok. Yes. Her mom and sister just arrived. Me, Tyrone and Kroy are waiting in the lobby of the emergency room to see when they are going to put Josh in a room. There is bad phone reception in the ER, so I came out to call you."

"You, Kroy and Tyrone – all in the same room? This is going to be interesting. I'm on my way," Kendra hung up and continued downtown.

Sherita hadn't even noticed that she was sitting in between her ex-husband and her new husband while waiting in the lobby. However, Tracy's mom, Alberta Jackson, had no tactful way of highlighting the obvious.

"Well, I'm not sure what to call you now-a-days gurl! Look at you, gorgeous as ever in between both of these two fine ass men you got. Tracy told me you'd gotten remarried. Said you had some new fancy name an all. Something French and rich sounding. So, what should we call you now? Or do you still go by Miz Coleman?" Alberta asked with intrigue.

Embarrassed, Sherita looked from side-to-side and was literally sitting in the middle of the two men in her life that she loved the most. Looking up at the ceiling, she thought, "Lord, why me?"

Tyrone and Kroy both felt the tension mounting and shifted in their seats a bit but elected to let Sherita handle this line of questioning.

"Ms. Jackson. I didn't recognize you," Sherita said coyly.

"Ummhmm, that was the same thing you said a few weeks ago when I saw you in the parking lot of the Family Dollar."

"I'm sorry. I am usually just not paying much attention. I really need to get better at that."

"So, what is yo new last name? What should I call you?"

"My new name is LaBeauf, but…"

"La- who?"

"Umm, please, just call me Sherita. It's really not a problem."

Sherita was trying to wiggle through this awkward moment when Kendra walked up – just in time.

"Sher! Oh my God, I got here as quickly as I could. Where is Josh? What are they saying? Is everything OK?"

Kendra was going a mile-a-minute, completely discounting Alberta standing right next to her. She leaned over and hugged Sherita and followed suit accordingly with Kroy and then Tyrone. In an instant, she sensed there was something wacky taking place.

Looking around she asked, "What's wrong with y'all?"

"Hi, I'm Alberta! Tracy's momma. I was just congratulating Mz. LaBoon on her new husband," Alberta said as she extended her hand to shake Kendra's hand.

Looking around with a confused look at Sherita and then to Kroy and Tyrone, who both looked as if they had to shit and trying desperately to hold it in, Kendra says, "I'm sorry? Mz. LaBoon? Who da'hell is that?"

"Well, that's ah..."

"Ah, Kendra, this is Tracy's mom. You know, Josh's girlfriend?" Sherita tried to save the environment from what was surely about to be a comic-relief moment.

"Oh! This her momma?" Kendra was in shock.

Kroy and Tyrone both stood at the same time to head for the cafeteria.

"Ah, Sher... my man Kroy and I are gonna go find some food and possibly some liquor," Tyrone said sarcastically.

"Yeah, we will be back shortly, mon amour. Would you like me to bring you something?" Kroy asked his wife as he leaned in to kiss her cheek.

"Ummph, I don't think I've had the pleasure of meeting you," Alberta said as she gazed at Kroy and extended her hand.

"Hi, I'm Alberta."

"Umm, I am, umm, Mr. LaBoon," Kroy said trying hard not to burst into laughter.

Meanwhile, Tyrone lost control and rushed down the hall bursting with laughter.

Embarrassed and completely confused, Sherita just sat back down in the chair shaking her head from side-to-side. Kendra needed the burst of laughter, she sat down next to Sherita with that "girl-this-yo'-shit" kind of look on her face.

"Well, it's nice to meet you, Mr. LaBoon," Alberta said.

"Likewise. Now, if you all will excuse me, I believe my man Ty and I are headed to the liquor store…I mean, the sundry shop."

As Sherita sat trying to get it all back on track, she hadn't even thought about calling Alana. And although Josh was OK, she would still want to know what was going on here at home. As she dialed the number, she gently put her hand on Kendra's and laid her head on her shoulder in appreciation for her love and support.

"Hey, Lan it's Mom. When you get this message, give me a call. Thanks."

Sherita hung up after she left the voicemail message.

"So, where have you been all day, Missy?" Sherita asked Kendra with intensity.

"What you mean? Where have I been? Where have you been all day?" Kendra asked back, trying to turn the attention back to Sherita.

She wasn't ready to share her news just yet. She really hadn't had time to process it and besides, she really wanted to have a discussion with Rico. Just as the two friends were about to start their conversation, the surgeon came into the waiting room with news on Tracy.

"Ms. Jackson?"

"Yeah, that's me," Alberta said as she and Tracy's sister stood to greet the doctor.

Sherita and Kendra stood as well so they could hear the information, and out of respect.

"Hello ma'am. I am Dr. Shawn. I am the head surgeon who worked on your daughter. First, let me say she is doing fine and made it through surgery very well. She did suffer quite a bit of internal injuries and a few broken ribs. Your daughter is very lucky to be alive and lucky that the young man in the car with her reacted as quickly as he did upon impact in stabilizing her head. I don't even think he realized what he was doing at the time, but he essentially saved her life."

"Lord Jesus! Lord Jesus! Lord Jesus!" Alberta screamed to the top of her lungs as she shimmied around in a circle with tears streaming down her face.

"Thank you, Jesus! Thank you!" she continued to shout.

"Now, ma'am, I will say that the next 48 hours will still be critical. She will remain in ICU during that time with round-the-clock monitoring, and we will make sure she is on track before we move her to a regular room. However, there is one more thing. Your daughter was about 6 weeks pregnant, and we were not able to save the fetus," Dr. Shawn said.

"PREGNANT!!" everyone yelled out loud simultaneously looking like they had been hit with a brick.

"Well, judging by the reaction of the group, I would assume that none of you knew about this?"

"Oh Lord, Oh Lord!" Alberta kept praying as she sat in the nearest chair.

"Is she going to be OK doctor?" Sherita asked with concern.

"Yes ma'am, she should be fine. There was quite a bit of damage to her uterus and, therefore, pregnancy down the line may be challenging, but she is young, and she can have greater discussions with her OB/GYN should she choose to."

"OK, thank you. When can we see her?" Sherita asked.

"She is in recovery now and she should be there for at least 45 minutes to an hour while they prepare a room for her in ICU. We will have someone come back down and let you all know as soon as we move her and when you can see her."

"Thank you."

Just as Dr. Shawn headed up the hall, Kroy and Tyrone were headed back around the corner.

"Hey. What'd the doctor say?" Tyrone immediately asked Sherita. "Ummm, Tracy made it through surgery successfully. She did suffer lots of internal damage and it seems as though because of Josh's quick thinking in stabilizing her head immediately following the impact, he may have saved her life," Sherita was talking a mile-a-minute.

"Oh thank God," Tyrone responded.

"Yeah, thank God – but…."

"But what?"

"Well, according to the doctor, Tracy was 6 weeks pregnant," Sherita said calmly.

"Huh? Come again? Did you just say pregnant?" Tyrone was stunned.

"Yes Ty, I said pregnant."

"Did you know anything about this? What the hell has been going on over at your house, Sherita?" Tyrone was yelling in an accusatory tone.

"What? What the hell are you insinuating Tyrone? Do you think I knew about this? Hell, I am just as shocked as you are," Sherita said in disbelief at her ex-husband's accusations.

"Hold on! Hold on! Now Tyrone, you are dead wrong for thinking that Sher would keep something like this from you if she knew about it. Now Josh is a grown man at 19 and he is not only old enough to be having sex, hell, he is old enough to tell his own news! So, you need to just calm down and you both need to talk to Josh and find out what is going on," Kendra chimed in. She surprised everyone with her sensible voice of reasoning.

Infuriated, Tyrone looked at the two women standing before him, and in a haste, headed down the corridor to the ER where Josh was waiting to be put in a room. Giving each other that "oh shit" look Kendra and Sherita both shot down the hall behind him.

"Son, we need to talk," Tyrone announced as he burst into the space behind the privacy curtain.

"Dad? Hey mom, hey Aunt Kendra," Josh was a bit groggy as he greeted everyone standing around him.

Kroy entered and stood next to Sherita as they all surrounded Josh's bed.

"Son, is there anything you need to tell us?" Tyrone continued.

"Josh, sweetie, we just spoke with the doctor and Tracy made it through surgery successfully. He also commented that if it had not been for your quick thinking, she may not have made it," Sherita tried desperately to make this conversation painless.

"Oh, thank God. Mom, I was so scared," Josh said with a hint of tears in his eyes.

"I called her to see if she could give me a ride home from work since I wasn't feeling well, and just as we were turning out of the mall, this car seemed like it came out of nowhere and slammed into us," Josh recalled. "Mom I was so scared, I didn't know what was going on, I didn't know what to do."

"I know sweetie. You did what you knew to do and that was to react immediately, and we are so proud of you for that," Sherita said as she comforted her son.

"Son, did you know that Tracy was pregnant?" Tyrone asked bluntly.

"What? Pregnant? How? When? No, Dad, I had no idea!" Josh's sincere shock was proof enough that he didn't have a clue.

If it was one thing Sherita and Tyrone knew about their children, it was the ability to tell when they were lying about something. The Coleman's had always instituted an open-door policy with Josh and Alana and worked diligently to make them comfortable enough to talk to them about anything. And while the shock of a baby would be gravely disappointing, the hope would be that they would have the courage to share it and not keep it a secret.

"Honey, according to the doctor, Tracy suffered severe internal damage along with a few broken ribs. Although she will be OK and should make a full recovery, it was also revealed that she was 6 weeks pregnant," Sherita continued.

"I had no idea. ... Oh my God," Josh was trying to process it all.

"Mom, I promise, I had no idea. She has been acting really strange lately and somewhat distant, but I've been working a lot and just figured she was pissed with me for not being able to spend as much time with her. Dad, I swear – I wore a jimmy every single time and there wasn't ever any slip ups."

Josh felt like he was rambling on and on. It all seemed so surreal. Why wouldn't Tracy tell him she was pregnant? His head was spinning. He felt like he had let his parents down. Just as Josh tried to sit up in the bed to speak again, Sherita's cellphone started ringing and the nurse entered the room.

"Hello everyone. I am Shannon, your nurse, and I need to check his vitals as we prepare to move him to a room upstairs.

I am going to have to ask everyone except his parents to leave the room for a minute."

Kroy and Kendra looked at each other and moved out of the way.

"Nephew, I love you and I will be right outside the entire time, OK? Don't worry, all of this will work itself out. You just focus on getting well, so we can bring you home, OK?" Kendra said as she leaned in to kiss Josh's forehead.

"Thanks Aunt Kendra. Love you, too."

Sherita handed the phone to Kendra, it was a missed call from Alana. Tyrone and Sherita looked at each other with uncertainty. Surely there would need to be some explanation for this unexplained pregnancy, however, it would have to wait until Tracy was well enough to speak about it.

"Josh, would you like some ice water?" asked nurse Shannon.

"Yes, thank you. Umm, when can I eat?"

"We will be moving you in the next half-hour upstairs to a room to keep you overnight for observation. Once you get upstairs, I will make a note in your chart for them to have some food brought up to you. Will that work?" she asked.

"Yeah, I guess I have no other choice. Thank you."

"OK, well, all of your vitals seem OK. You did take a pretty nice hit to the head, so you may start to experience a slight headache once the pain medications wear off. If so, just let us know and we will get you more ibuprofen. I will be back to get you as soon as the room is ready. Oh, and I will bring you some water right back."

Tyrone was the first to step to the side of his son's bed. He loved his children beyond anything else in life. He became a bit overwhelmed at the thought - realizing the only other person he ever loved as much as Josh and Alana was Sherita. As he glanced at her from across the room, he quickly realized he needed to get it together.

"Son, I am very proud of you. Your actions today proved heroic in helping to essentially save Tracy's life."

Sherita tried desperately to hold back tears. She was just so grateful and relieved that Josh was OK. She was just as concerned with what future discussions would be surrounding this unknown baby.

"J, your dad is right. We are very proud of you. I don't know what I would do if that were you in that operating room. I would probably be scrubbed in and standing next to 'em, giving them step-by-step instructions on how to take care of my baby," Sherita said with a chuckle.

"I can only imagine, Mom," Josh smiled.

"And the crazy thing is she is serious," chimed Tyrone.

As the family lovingly enjoyed a much-needed laugh break, they were pleasantly interrupted by Kendra.

"Are those laughs I hear coming from this area?" Kendra said with a huge smile as she stuck her head in the room.

"Sorry to interrupt, Sher, wanted to bring the phone back and encourage you to please call Alana. I just spoke with her, and she needs to know that Josh is OK."

Kendra respectfully smiled and winked at Josh as she retreated back to the waiting room.

Realizing he, too, had several missed calls from Alana, Tyrone gave Sherita that look of "call her now before she loses it".

"Mom! Oh my God! I am freaking out, what is going on? What happened? Where is Josh? Is he going to be OK? Is Dad there? Can he call and book me a flight tonight? I need to come home and check on Josh! Mom! Mom!" Alana was frantic.

Sherita couldn't get a word in edgewise. Alana was extremely emotional and yelling and crying almost uncontrollably. She was desperately trying to calm her down to get her questions answered.

"Lan! Lan, honey, calm down! Stop! Stop! Let me talk please!"

"Honey, first of all, calm down. You are going to start to hyperventilate in a minute. Now, your brother is fine. He has a few bumps and bruises – but he is fine. They are going to move him to a room shortly and only keep him overnight for observation. And yes, your dad is here with us and no, I don't think he is going to book you a flight to come home tonight. I think we've got it all under control," Sherita spoke calmly to help soothe Alana's concerns.

"Oh My God, Mom – I was so worried. OK. Can I speak with him?"

"It's OK, sweetie. I know you are just worried about your brother. Now, who would you like to speak with? Josh or your dad?"

"Josh first."

Handing Josh the phone, Sherita gave Tyrone that "that is yo' child" kind of look as she smiled with pride at the level of love the sister and brother shared for one another.

"Hello."

"Hey lil' bro – how you feel?" Alana said in a much calmer tone than the one she had with her mom on the phone.

"Hey Lan. I am better now that you're on the phone. I'm OK."

"Ahh, I was about to lose my mind, not knowing what was going on. How is Tracy? Aunt Kendra said she had to go into emergency surgery."

"Yeah, she wasn't wearing a seatbelt. As far as I know, she is going to be OK. I am waiting on someone to get me an update soon."

"Well good. I am sure she will be OK. Listen, you get some rest, and I am going to be home in a couple of weeks to check on you, OK?"

"OK. Thanks Lan. You know I love you, right?"

"You don't love me! You just love my SWAG!!!" she said laughing out loud in the phone.

"True dat, Sis. True dat," Josh said trying to follow the theme of the discussion.

"OK, let me holler at Daddy."

Handing the phone to Tyrone, Josh looked tired, confused and angry.

"How's my baby girl?" Tyrone said cheerfully as he took the phone.

"Hey daddy! I am much better now. I thought for a minute I was going to have to activate my emergency money fund to come see about Josh."

"I bet you did. Honey, your brother is alright. He is pretty tough, he is a Coleman you know," Tyrone said with a chuckle.

"Tough, Daddy? Really? This is Josh we are talking about. Remember, the same kid that wore a Tweety Bird band-aid on a barely visible cut on his face from shaving for nearly a week!"

Laughing at the thought, Tyrone said: "You got me on that one, sweetie."
"So, everything good with you up there?"

"Yes Daddy, I am good. OK, well, I won't keep you – I will call to check on you guys tomorrow. But please Daddy, promise me that you will call me if anything changes – OK?"

"OK. I promise. I love you, Alana."

"Tell her I love her, too, and I will call her later tonight!" Sherita chimed in.

"Mom says love you as well."

"OK – love you guys, too, Daddy. Bye."

As Alana hung up the phone, she had tears in her eyes. Her little brother was in Atlanta in the hospital following a car accident with her parents worried sick, and here she was in New York in the CVS drug store sitting in the aisle comparing home pregnancy tests. What will she do if this thing is positive? How will she tell her parents? How is she going to tell Rico?

Chapter 8

Rico knew he was going to have to deal with his wife, Sabrina, after having stayed out all night. He really hadn't planned for it to end up that way, but hey – when it's good, it's good and you just can't stop.

His relationship with Alana was just so easy. Outside of her acting like an immature brat every now and then, he liked the fact that he was in total control of her. She was such a pretty girl and, he did enjoy spending time with her. His house was quiet as he came through the front door.
Relieved, he put his keys on the coffee table walked into the family room and picked up the remote to turn on the TV. Finally, a calm space. He headed toward the kitchen when all of a sudden, a bullet raced past his head.

"What the hell is wrong with you, Sabrina? What are you doing? You almost shot me in the head!"

"Consider that a warning shot ASSHOLE! The next one will be intentional!"

Baw! Baw! Baw! Sabrina quickly unloaded another 3 rounds from the small handgun trimmed in pink. With perfect aim and determination on her face she was out for blood and that blood was that of her husband of 10 years - Rico.

Rico instinctively dived to the kitchen floor and rolled under the table to attempt to shield himself. He couldn't believe what was happening. Sabrina had instantly turned their home into a battlefield, and he was the only target in sight. He could hear police sirens in the distance as he attempted to plead with his wife.

"Sabrina! What the hell are you doing? Put down the gun Sabrina before you do something you're going to regret!" he yelled from under the table.

"REGRET!? REGRET! Right now, the only thing I regret Rico is marrying yo' sorry, lying and cheating ass!" she was infuriated.

"Baby, listen! I can explain! I know I fucked up! But I promise you baby – it's over! It's all over!" Rico pleaded desperately.

The police arrived banging on the door. "Open up! NYPD! Please drop your weapon!"

"NOT BEFORE I KILL THIS MOTHERFUCKER! Officer, I hope you brought someone from the M.E.'s office, 'cause you gon need a body bag for his ass when it is all said and done up in here!"

"Ma'am, listen, you don't want to do this. Now, I don't know what he has done, but I am sure we can work it all out if you just drop your weapon and step outside."

The officer worked diligently to convince Sabrina to handle this in a calmer manner.

Nearly 6 cop cars and a dozen officers were out front of the brownstone that Rico and Sabrina shared for the past 6 years. The neighbors were gathered outside trying to see what was going on and hoping that she hadn't already killed her apparent hostage.

After the first shot, a neighbor across the street immediately dialed 911 reporting shots fired.

Upon a count down, the police proceeded to break through the front door. Once inside, they could see the back of Sabrina standing over the kitchen table with her handgun pointed ready to shoot to kill a visibly frightened Rico under the table.

"Ma'am, this is Officer Hollis. I am slowly approaching you from behind and would advise that you lower your weapon immediately. Do you understand me?"

Shaking her head in agreement, Sabrina was in tears. She had dark circles under her eyes from lack of sleep, mascara smeared across her cheeks and disheveled hair that hadn't been combed in days. She slowly lowered the gun as she

turned to face the officer. With a look of utter disgust on her face, she just shook her head from side-to-side as she walked toward Officer Hollis. She handed him the gun and broke down in tears on the floor. Officer Hollis secured the weapon and sought to console this woman scorned.

As he tended to Sabrina, his team rushed in to ensure that Rico was OK. Although none of the shots had reached their intended target, he was very nervous and very shaken up by the altercation.

"Sir, are you hit anywhere? Sir?"

In complete dissolution, Rico was speechless. Sabrina had never reacted this way with him in all the years he'd known her.

"Umm, yeah. I mean no. I am not hit anywhere."

"Sir, we have an ambulance out front to check you out just in case, please come with me," the officer said.

Rico couldn't take his eyes off his wife who was sitting on the floor talking to the officer as he stepped across her and headed out the front door. The scene out front seemed like something from a movie with cop cars, spectators and even local media trucks on hand. As he made it to the ambulance, he wasn't sure what had just happened.

"Sir, my name is Officer Polk, and this is my partner Officer Arnold. We need to ask you a few questions about what just took place here. I assume you know the suspect?"

"Umm, yeah. She's, my wife."

"Any reason why she would open fire on you the way that she did?"

"She is upset with me. We've been having some problems lately. And she recently found out that I was having an affair and..."

"What types of problems had you been having, outside of this recent affair?"

"We've been trying for a while to have a baby and she has had two miscarriages and there has just been a lot of stress on our relationship the past year or so and things just have gotten progressively worse."

As Rico found himself answering questions surrounding Sabrina's actions, he could see them bringing her out of the house in handcuffs and escorting her to a squad car.

"Hey. Where is she going? Where are they taking her?" he said frantically.

"Sir, she is going down to the precinct to be booked into custody for attempted murder."

"Murder? What? No! She.... she didn't mean it. Can, I go with her?" Both officers looked at each other with the "classic idiot" look and proceeded to assist Rico with getting his stuff.

"Sir, you can meet us down at the precinct and work out the logistics there. We will need to take a formal statement from you at that time and determine if whether or not you wish to file charges."

"File charges? No, I don't want to file charges! Just, let my wife go – we can work this out."

The squad car left with Sabrina in the back headed downtown. Local news reporters were surrounding Rico as he emerged from the ambulance, spewing questions about what had happen in their home. With no comment, he quickly rushed inside his house to grab his wallet and his keys.

He had to fix this.

Reporters hovered around his front door.

"Sir, can you tell us what happened inside the house with you and your wife earlier?"

"Is it true that your wife just tried to gun you down after learning of an apparent affair?"

"Do you plan to press charges against your wife for attempting to kill you?"

Rico, pressed his way past the crowd, not answering any of the limitless questions. He needed to get to the police station to get Sabrina out of this mess. This was all his fault. He shouldn't have taken her on this emotional rollercoaster.

As he headed toward the subway station, he realized he left his cellphone. Surely, by now, his family had seen what was happening on the news. They would just have to wait. Right now, he needed to get to his wife.

The jail was cold and uninviting. Sabrina had never been in such a place in her life. Looking around the room, she suddenly felt ill and didn't feel safe. Officer Hollis offered her a cup of black coffee as he directed her to sit in a row of chairs that resembled the line at the DMV. The room was swarming with men and women in uniform and people who looked like common criminals. As she peered around the room, she noticed a man lying in the corner who looked like he was intoxicated and had urinated all over himself.

"Mrs. Harris, if you would, have a seat here and someone will call you up shortly for fingerprinting and to take your picture," Officer Hollis said.

Still in handcuffs, Sabrina sat with her hands in her lap. She barely noticed the seemingly older lady sitting next to her.

"Excuse me, princess, you wouldn't happen to have a smoke, would you?" the lady asked.

Sabrina looked around the room as if to see who exactly the lady was speaking to.

"Yeah, I'm talking to you, honey. Got a smoke?"

"No. I don't smoke," she replied dryly.

"What'd they get you on? Jay-walkin' or something?" the lady said with a light chuckle.

"Attempted murder," Sabrina said calmly as she looked the lady in her eyes.

"DAMN princess! I never woulda pegged you for a killa or nothing. Who'd you grapple wit?"

Irritated by this exchange, the reality of her own words had just hit Sabrina. She was in deep shit, and she wasn't sure how she was going to get out of this one.

"I tried to kill my husband," she said as she stared at an apparent blood stain in the floor.

"Sabrina Harris!"

Startled at the sound of her name, Sabrina looked up to see a small-framed lady in uniform holding a clipboard waving in her direction.

"Are you Sabrina Harris?"

"Yes."

"Step to the side right here. I am going to remove your handcuffs to fingerprint you. We will record each finger starting with your left hand. Once you have completed this task, you will use the wet wipes in the basket to clean off the ink. You then will proceed to the next window where your photo will be taken and, afterward, we will collect some additional information from you. Do you understand?"

"Yes."

Once she made it through the booking process, Sabrina was taken to a locker room where she was asked to remove all articles of clothing including undergarments. She was given a bright orange jumpsuit, a pair of flip flops and a paper pack of underwear and bra. She was instructed to list all of her personal items on a sheet of paper and seal it in a large plastic bag. Once she turned in her belongings, Officer Hollis came in the room.

"Ma'am, before we take you down, we would like a minute to ask you some additional questions. Is that OK?"

"Yeah, sure."

Officer Hollis escorted her to a small interrogation room where it resembled everything you see on television: small table with four chairs and a huge window that you couldn't see into the opposite side. Sabrina was amazed at how secluded it all seemed, but yet still felt violated knowing that people were watching her every move and could hear her breathing.

"Please, have a seat," Officer Hollis offered. "Ma'am, what happened?"

"Um, I don't know. I just lost it. He didn't come home last night, and this has become a pattern for the past year or so. Late nights. Claiming he's working with his students. Strange numbers in his phone from a 404-area code. So, I followed him. I seen him leave the hotel room. I…. I," Sabrina just rambled on for what seemed like an eternity.

"How long have you had the gun?"

"Two months."

"I wasn't really going to kill him. I love his dumb ass too much to do that. I just wanted to scare him. Make him understand my pain and frustration."

"Has something been going on between the two of you? Fighting?"

"We've been trying to have a baby for the past year and a half. I have a weak cervix and therefore have had several miscarriages.

Rico says he is OK with it and that he loves me, but deep down inside, I know he really wants a child. And I can't give him that. Part of me doesn't blame him for cheating. Hell, I probably would do the same thing if I were with someone who couldn't make babies. But I love him, and I don't know what my life would be like without him," she said as tears fell from her eyes.

"Ma'am, I'm sorry about the loss you've suffered and even more sorry that your husband appears to be an insensitive bastard. But you've committed a very serious crime and attempted murder is punishable by a lofty prison sentence. I am going to let you stay in here for as long as I can. However, I highly recommend you call a lawyer. You're going to need one."

"Do I get a phone call?"

"Yes. You do."

The last time Rico had been to the county jail was nearly three years ago when he went to bail out one of his students for disorderly conduct. Who knew his next visit would be on behalf of his wife? He was nervous for her and what the charges would be, he knew that at this point, despite his unwillingness to press charges, the prosecutor would be in full control of the situation. He waited anxiously in line at the information desk.

"Next please."

"Ahh, yes – I need to bail my wife out of jail."

"Name?"

"Sabrina Harris."

"Sir looks like there has not been a bail set for your wife at this time. Her court date isn't scheduled until Monday morning at 9:00 a.m. She is still going through central booking and being held on attempted murder charges, which means it will be at least 24 hours before she is even able to receive visitors. Here is an information card with an automated number – call it in 24 hours and enter this case number and it will provide you with updates."

The lady handed Rico a white business card with supporting information listed on the front. He was dazed, shocked and terrified that Sabrina would not be able to leave jail that night.

"Sir, do you have any additional questions?"

"Umm, no. I mean, yes. By chance can I speak with Officer Hollis?" In all of the chaos, Rico had managed to remember the name of the officer who had gotten his wife to release her weapon. He hoped that if he could speak to the Officer, maybe he could shed some light on Sabrina's situation.

"Let me see if he is still here. Please have a seat in the waiting area and I will try to locate him."

Alana woke up in a daze at the sound of the buzzing cellphone on her nightstand. As she opened her eyes, she realized that her nap had turned into a full night's sleep. When she picked up the phone, she noticed several missed calls and text messages from Bella.

"Hello."

"Alana! Girl, where have you been? I've been calling you all night!" Bella was loud.

"Belle, I have been home asleep. What's going on? Everything OK?"

"Apparently, you haven't watched the news or seen today's paper?"

"No, I haven't what's going on?" Alana asked as she sat on the side of the bed feeling for the TV remote.

"Well, I hate to be the one to tell you this Lan but looks like your "Mr. Married Professor" has been found out by wifey. She tried to kill him last night in their home. It is all over the news and everyone on campus is talking about it."

"Huh? What are you saying, Bella? Is Rico…. dead?"

"Girl, no. Lucky for his ass his wife is a bad shot, but, unfortunately for her, she is in county lockup!"

"Shit! Belle, I will call you back."

Alana hung up the phone hurriedly. Still looking for the remote, she thumbed through the missed calls in her phone. She saw one missed call from Rico and a couple from her mom. She couldn't believe she'd slept so long but was exhausted from everything the day before. The last thing she remembered was coming home and taking the pregnancy test she'd bought at drugstore.

Suddenly, she remembered the test and jumped up to rush to the bathroom. Nervous, she looked at the stick lying on the counter.

"Oh shit…. it's positive."

This has got to be a bad dream!

Chapter 9

Tyrone woke up with a crook in his neck realizing he had spent the night in an uncomfortable chair inside Josh's hospital room. There was a familiarity within his spirit as he looked down to see that his ex Sherita's head was nestled ever so gently on his chest where she'd fallen asleep as well. Just as he started to shift in his seat, he looked up into the burning eyes of his wife, Felicia. He hadn't called home since leaving for the hospital yesterday and instantly understood that she must have been worried sick about him and his son.

"Oh, I'm sorry Ty – I must have dozed off to sleep," Sherita said with a groan as she sat up in the chair.

Looking around the room she first looked at Josh who had an interesting look on his face as he diverted his eyes toward Felicia standing in the door. Sensing immediate tension in the room, she turned to look at Felicia.

"Umm, good morning, Felicia. I know what this must look like, but…"

"Save it! I don't want to hear your explanation for being all hugged up with my husband!" she was furious.

"Felicia, baby - it's really not what you think," Tyrone tried to explain.

"REALLY? Then what the hell should I think, Ty? You left in a haste yesterday afternoon, with little to no information on Josh's condition. I have been calling your cell phone all night trying to find out something, hell anything but no answer!

I prayed all night, thinking that everything was going to be fine and that you would call as soon as you knew something. Hmph, just my luck, things look like they were GREAT! I rushed down here to find the two of you all hugged up like one big happy family."

"Felicia, it really isn't that at all. Sherita and I have been up all night long making sure that Josh is OK, and we must've fallen asleep in the process. I promise, it is nothing, nothing at all," Tyrone was trying to maintain a calm tone of voice.

Sherita stood and walked toward Josh in the bed. She figured it would be best to let Tyrone handle the situation with his wife.

"Well, Tyrone if you and that BITCH want to be together…"

"Whoa! Who you callin a BITCH?" Josh rose up out of the bed.

"BITCH?" Sherita yelled turning around to face Felicia.

"Look here heffa, you know like I know you got less than 20 seconds to take that shit outside and find yourself before I show you what a real BITCH looks like; and I guarantee Tyrone won't be able to save yo' ass!" Sherita went from 0 to 60 in a matter of seconds.

"FELICIA!" Tyrone yelled.

"Are you serious? My son is lying in a hospital bed, and you walk up in here in a jealous rage because you think you saw something that I am telling you is nothing?

Then you go to spewing names out at my ex-wife and expect that you are in the right? STEP OUTSIDE NOW!" Tyrone was infuriated.

"Yeah, you better take that shit outside lady, before I give you something to be upset about. Calling my Momma, a bitch. We ain't havin' that! Not today!" Josh retaliated.

"Josh! Honey, calm down! Calm down, get back in the bed. It's OK," Sherita said.

Just as the nurses came rushing into the room, right behind them was Kendra and Kroy.

"Mi'Amore, is everything OK?"

"What in da' hell is going on in here?" Kendra asked ready to fight.

"Honey, I'm fine," Sherita said calmly.

"That crazy Felicia gone come in here and saw Mom laying on Dad's chest and started yelling and screaming like she on crack or something calling my mom a BITCH," Josh blurted out.

"BITCH?!" Kendra had a raised eyebrow.

"Wait, what? Lying on your dad's chest?" Kroy was confused.

"Honey, I can explain."

"Kendra, it's fine. Tyrone took her up the hall to talk to her," Sherita didn't want the situation to escalate any further than it already had.

"Yeah, he better take that weave-wearing wart up the hall and calm her ass down. She better be glad I wasn't in the room when she decided to display her illustrious vocabulary, calling somebody a BITCH and what not. I got a BITCH for ha' ass!"

Kendra was heated. She didn't care much for Felicia anyway and looked for any excuse to give her a piece of her mind.

"Young man, are you OK?" the nurse asked Josh.

"Yes ma'am, I'm OK."

"OK, good. I need you to stay in the bed. You don't want to risk your IV coming out and causing problems."

"Yes. I'm sorry. I will stay here," Josh complied.

"For everyone else in the room, I don't know exactly what is going on in here, but you are going to have to conduct yourselves in a more respectful manner or else I will have security remove you from the premises. The doctor will be in shortly to evaluate Josh to see if he is well enough to be released today. I am going to ask that only his parents remain in the room until then. Do you understand me?"

The nurse was pleasant, but stern. Kroy, Kendra and Sherita each nodded in agreement. Sherita sat back down on the double chair rubbing her temples. Kendra felt a sense of nausea and instantly ran into the restroom behind her. Kroy stood in silence, looking at his wife deciding to wait until later to ask his questions out of respect for her son.

Tyrone came back in the room with a look of anger and frustration. He walked over to Josh and kissed him on the forehead.

"Sorry son. I love you. I'm gonna call and check on you later, OK?"

"Dad, you leavin'?" Josh asked with a look of confusion.

"Yeah son. I need to go. I'm sure your mom will call me if anything changes or if she needs me."

Kroy and Sherita both looked at each other speechless. Kroy stood to shake Tyrone's hand and do the bruh-man's hug. Tyrone placed his hand on Sherita's shoulder.

"Keep me posted on my boy, OK?"

"Ty is everything alright? You guys don't have to leave, we are all adults here you know," Sherita said with concern.

"Who's leavin'?" Kendra asked as she emerged from the bathroom.

Without addressing the question, Tyrone just looked at Kendra and headed out the door. He felt disgusted at Felicia's behavior and embarrassed by the whole incident.

He and Sherita have always had a very special bond and connection even beyond the parenting of their kids. He knew it would be a difficult journey to navigate once either of them decided to remarry and bring someone else into the equation. Most exes can't stand to be in the same room with one another, let alone be able to share strictly platonic moments of comfort with each other.

CHAPTER 10

Tracy hadn't seen Josh since the accident. The few days she spent in the hospital seemed like weeks. When she finally became conscious, she was devastated at the news that she lost the baby.

"They say you should be able to go home later today, honey. Isn't that good news?" Alberta asked.

Tracy hadn't really said much and was consumed with the thought of Josh and how he was doing? As Alberta adjusted the pillow behind her daughter's head, the nurse walked in.

"Hello, I am Giselle, and I will be preparing your discharge papers for you today. I know you're excited about going home. Now, the doctor has prescribed two different antibiotics to ensure that you don't develop an infection, and an 800-milligram pain reliever that should only be taken as needed. Do not consume any alcoholic beverages while on the medication and do not drive or operate any motor vehicles. Be sure to follow up with your primary care physician in 7 days. Do you have any questions?"

"No ma'am, I think we got it all," Alberta chimed. She was ready to take her daughter home and put all of this behind her.

"Good. Go ahead and get your stuff together and someone will be up within the hour with a wheelchair to escort you to your car. Good luck to you and wishing you a speedy recovery."

As the orderly wheeled Tracy down the hall, Alberta was in tow with all her belongings, balloons and get-well-soon cards. They waited anxiously on the elevator only to discover Josh and Sherita inside once the doors opened.

"Why didn't you tell me you were pregnant?" Josh asked immediately as they got on the elevator.

"Look, I don't think this is the appropriate time to discuss…" Alberta jumped to her daughter's defense.

"With all due respect Ms. Alberta, nobody asked you to think," Josh was livid.

"Son," Sherita said as she grabbed Josh's arm.

"I don't want to talk right now Josh," Tracy said nervously.

"Well then I guess you don't want to talk ever. Pregnant by some other dude and don't even have the decency or respect to tell me. Damn near get me killed and I have to find out from my folks! What kind of shit is that?!"

Shocked and amazed by Josh's outburst, Tracy had streams of tears rolling down her face. She knew she should have told Josh sooner, but she just didn't know how.

As the doors of the elevator opened, Sherita pushed past the wheelchair to run after her son, who had darted out before the doors had fully opened. She understood how disappointed and hurt he must be feeling, but she also realized that at this point, she was going to have to let him deal with it in his own time. Josh sat down on the bench outside the emergency room with his head in his hands.

"I'll go bring the car around son."

The drive home was quiet. Josh really wasn't in the mood to talk and Sherita understood. As she fumbled with the radio, she finally landed on a song "No Rhyme or No Reason" by George Duke that brought back memories.

"Ain't it the truth," she thought to herself.

Sherita hadn't spoken with Tyrone since yesterday's debacle in the hospital room with Felicia. She felt bad that it all transpired the way it did. Kroy hadn't brought it up yet, but something deep within her told her that it wouldn't be long before that conversation took place. She really didn't want him to feel as if there was still any love connection between her and Tyrone outside of their relationship for their kids. Kroy had been quieter than usual and so perhaps she needed to bring it up first.

As Sherita and Josh pulled into the driveway, they were greeted with a huge welcome home banner that Kroy had hung on the front of the house. Noticing both Tyrone and Kendra's car in the yard, Sherita was a bit worried, since she didn't have a clue what was going on.

"Mom, what's going on?" Josh asked as they got out of the car.

"Honestly, son I don't know. After yesterday, I figured I would just get you and bring you home myself and keep down confusion. But let's go inside and see."

As soon as Josh opened the door, Alana jumped up from the kitchen table and yelled "SURPRISE!!"

"LAN!!!" he grabbed his sister with joy and hugged her tightly.

"Oh my God! When did you get here? I didn't know you were coming. I am so glad to see you."

He was rattling off a mile-a-minute.

Pleasantly surprised, Sherita reached out to hug her baby girl as well.

"Honey, how wonderful! When did you and your dad plan all of this?" Sherita asked looking at
Tyrone.

"Hey, it wasn't me," Tyrone said as he raised his hands in the air with a show of innocence.
"Huh?"

"No mom, it wasn't dad, it was Kroy!" Lan said with a huge smile on her face.

"Kroy called me and said that Josh was doing much better but that he felt that if my schedule permitted it would be very special for him if I came home for a couple of days. He arranged everything and I was on a flight out early this morning. Luckily, you were already planning to leave for the hospital early and so between he and Aunt Kendra, we made it all work," Lan explained excitedly.

"Wow! Thanks babe," Sherita said as she wrapped her arms around Kroy's neck and planted a loving kiss on his lips.

"Anything for you, Mi'Amore. I just wanted to brighten the mood a bit. The past few days in the hospital have been grueling on everyone, especially Josh. I thought it would brighten his day to see his sister for a few days." Kroy had scored some cool points with everyone in the room.

"Well, now that the family reunion is under way, what the hell do y'all have to eat up in here?" Kendra blurted out.

"There you go, always thinking about food! You need to be out walking around the block, you think we haven't noticed them few pounds you've put on," Tyrone said jokingly to Kendra.

"Shut'da hell up Ty! Aint nobody stuttin' you!"

Shaking her head in amusement, Sherita sat on Kroy's lap at the kitchen table and watched her family enjoy this happy moment.

As the evening drew to a close, Josh was grateful for the love and support of his family. The past few months truly seemed unbelievable in addition to what the events of the past few days had presented. He couldn't believe that Tracy could betray him in such a manner. What had he done to deserve such unjust treatment from her? The more he thought about it, the more he became upset. He decided he needed to just go to his room for a bit.

"Son, everything OK?" Tyrone asked as he watched Josh walk with a slight limp down the hall.

"Yeah Dad. I'm fine, just gonna lay down for a bit."

"OK. Well here, let me get a hug in. I guess I better head on home before another misinterpreted interaction ensues," he said trying to be funny.

The two shared a loving embrace that clearly demonstrated the respect and affection between them. Tyrone hadn't brought up the discussion regarding Tracy with his son, he felt he would give Josh the opportunity to talk about it in his own time. He understood how his son felt, having also experienced betrayal and deceit in his own life. As much as he loved Sherita, she'd once broken his heart and for a long time he didn't think he would ever open up and allow himself to love again. It was a difficult situation to be in and he hated to know that Josh would have to go through the emotional rollercoaster on his own.

After about 30 minutes, Alana decided to check on Josh.

Knock, knock, knock....

Alana tapped lightly on Josh's door.

"Josh? You sleep?" she asked as she pushed the door open slightly.

"Naw. Come on in."

"How you feelin'?"

"So, so… pride hurt more than anything," he said as he shrugged his shoulders.

"What does that mean?" Alana asked with a look of confusion as she sat down on the side of the bed.

Josh rolled over and laid his head in his sister's lap. It was in that moment that he realized he really did miss her. She had always been the only one that he could truly talk to.

"Lan, Tracy was pregnant."

"What!?" she said with a gasp.

"Yeah. Exactly what I said."

"You mean, you didn't know?"

"I didn't have a clue. I mean, we had been arguing quite a bit over the past month or so and I have been working a lot trying to save up to buy a new car, I just thought we were going through a rough patch," Josh opened up about his thoughts.

"So, when did she tell you she was pregnant?"

"That's just it. She didn't. I found out in the hospital when they apparently had to do emergency surgery on her to take the baby. Here I am laying in the hospital room worried sick about her and all of a sudden Mom and Dad come in and start asking me all these questions. Finally, Dad just came out and said it. He thought I knew about it and just hadn't told him and Mom, but I was just as shocked as they were. You know how they are about stuff like that and clearly if I was in that type of trouble, I would've called you or at the very least Aunt Kendra to figure it all out."

"Wow. Josh, I just don't know what to say," Alana was stunned at her brother's story. She didn't have a clue of any of the things that had transpired at the hospital; each time she and her mom talked she indicated that Josh was fine. All of a sudden, she felt sick to her stomach. Realizing that she was pregnant, how in the world would she tell her family. Especially now, with what Josh was going through?

"I hate her Lan! How could she do this to me?" Josh had tears in his eyes.

"Well, Josh, it seems as though you both have some level of responsibility for what happened. So how can you say you hate her?"

"Lan, the baby wasn't mine."

"Oh, shit!"

At a loss for words, Alana ran her hand across her little brother's head for some level of comfort.

"Have you talked to her?"

"I don't want to hear anything she has to say. Not only did she cheat on me, but she let another dude get her pregnant. There really isn't much more to discuss."

Chapter 11

Kendra couldn't wait to get in the house to get out of her shoes. Her feet were killing her. As of late it seemed as if she were constantly outgrowing her clothes. This whole pregnancy thing was going to be a problem. She wasn't going to be able to keep it a secret much longer. With everything that's been going on, she hadn't even told Sherita. She didn't want to tell her before having an opportunity to share the news with Rico. It had been more than a week and she hadn't heard from him. She had been so consumed with making sure Josh was OK she really hadn't thought much about the fact that he hadn't called.

Just as Kendra was coming in the door, she could hear the phone ringing.

"Hello…" she said out of breath.

"Just checking to see that you made it home OK," Sherita said on the other end.

"Girl yes! Glad to get out of them shoes. Damn, Jimmy Choo's cute, but hurt like hell! All that damn money, don't make no sense."

"Ha ha ha, girl you are a mess," Sherita laughed. "Thanks, Kendra, for all your support this past week. I really don't know what I would've done without you."

"Chile, you don't owe me no thanks. Josh and Alana are just as much my kids as they are yours, and if the Jimmy Choo was on the other foot, you would've done the same thing for me," she joked.

"I know. I know. Some days it blows my mind that he and Alana are all grown up and even having to deal with real life stuff. I mean, seriously a baby!? Wow, what would that have been like?"

"Hmph, it would've been you and that big head Tyrone beaming with pride after the initial shock at the fact that y'all were grandparents. But thank God it happened the way it did. Girl, Josh and Tracy didn't need no baby. Even if it wasn't his, that lil' fast-ass girl and her crazy-ass Momma probably would've schemed up some mess to get him caught up and stuck for the next 18 years. This situation may've been a blessing in disguise."

"Yeah, I guess you're right. I just feel bad for Josh that he has to deal with this type of stuff at such a young age. I mean, I think back to when we were in college and those days were tough emotionally."

"But those days were just that…. those days, these kids got their own path to travel. Luckily, for Josh, right now a baby isn't a part of his."

"Which is more than I can say for some," Kendra continued under her breath.

"What does that mean?" Sherita asked with a slight smirk on her face.

"Sher, I got something to tell you."

"OK."

Sitting on the tile floor in her kitchen with her back against the wall, Kendra's eyes filled with tears as she took a deep breath to prepare to share with her best friend her news of being pregnant.

Her emotions were so out of order that she wasn't sure why she wasn't happier about the idea. In a way, she was a bit embarrassed. After all, she'd only known Rico a short time, he lived in another state, and she really didn't know anything about him. Kendra steadied her thoughts as she took a deep breath to share her news and the other line clicked on the phone.

"Shit! Hold on. Someone is calling on the other line," Kendra said as she clicked over.

"Hello!"
"You have a collect call from the Nassau County Police Department in New York City. Do you accept the charges for the call?" the operator asked on the other end.

"What? A collect call from where? I think you've got the wrong number. I don't know nobody in Nassau County, N.Y." Kendra hung up.

"Sher, you there?"

"Yeah, I'm here. Who was that? What took so long?"

"Girl, wrong number. Somebody, calling with a collect call from Nassau County Jail in New York. Hell, not only do I not accept collect calls, I damn sho' ain't takin' no calls from jail! Anyway."

"Collect call? Umph," Sherita responded.

"So, what do you have to tell me?"

Kendra was nervous. The phone line clicked again.

"Dammit! Hold on!"

"Wait! Kendra, just call me back. I gotta go pee," Sherita blurted out.

Click… the phone line rung again.

"Pee? Girl, OK. I'll hit you back."

"Hello!"

Kendra was agitated at the second phone call and ready to give a piece of her mind to whomever kept calling. Just as the operator started again, Kendra's cellphone rang. It was Rico.
Hanging up the house phone without a second thought, she immediately pressed the green button on her cell.

"Well, well, well…. if it isn't Mr. Disappear himself," she said sarcastically.

"Kendra. I know. I know. There has just been a lot going on here lately and I've been dealing with lots of unexpected family drama," Rico replied.

"Hmph, family drama? I haven't talked to you in nearly a week. Surely you could've picked up the phone at least once and said Hey cat, dog, SOMETHING."

"Look, you're right. I apologize, I didn't call. But I am calling now, and we really need to talk," Rico wanted to end the relationship with Kendra. He knew that this was not going to work and given the events that had taken place over the past few days, his focus needed to be on his wife.

"You're right. We do need to talk. I have something to tell you," Kendra was nervous.

"OK. What's up?"

"Well. Ummm. The past few weeks have been really weird for me. I've really not been feeling my best and just not myself. I wasn't sure what was going on at first but then, I went to get checked out to see if maybe I was just anemic or something, because I didn't have any energy, "Kendra was rambling. "Rico, I'm pregnant."

There was a deafening silence on the other end of the phone. For a second, Kendra thought Rico had hung up.

"You, there?" she asked hesitantly.

"Pregnant?" Rico was speechless.

"Yeah…pregnant, as in with a baby."

"Are you sure? Is it mine?" Rico's mind was racing. This just can't be happening.

"Is it yours?" Kendra had an attitude. "What do you mean? Is it yours? Hell yeah, it's yours. Why would you even ask that dumb-ass question?"

"What do you mean, what do I mean? Hell, I don't know if I am the only guy you've been with. I am not in Atlanta with you 24-hours-a-day seven-days-a-week!" Rico said with an elevated tone in his voice.

"First of all, who the fuck you raising your voice at? Second of all, NEGRO for your information you are the ONLY motherfucker I been with. And trust me, I wouldn't choose to get knocked up by a brother in a whole 'nother state to whom I really don't know shit about any damn way," Kendra was pissed.

"OK. Look. What do you plan to do?" Rico was nervous. This is the last thing he needed was a pregnant chick in another state to be worried about; just his luck to go and get some woman pregnant that isn't his wife.

"You know what Rico, never fucking mind what I plan to do. It is obvious that you don't see yourself factoring into whatever that 'plan' may or may not be, so let me save you the trouble. Lose my damn phone number and forget you know me or anything about 'MY' baby. I don't need some bullshit ass brotha questioning my actions or acting with hesitation toward my unborn child; consider this your out. Kiss my ass!" Kendra clicked the off button on her cellphone.

Visibly upset by the conversation, she realized she was breathing heavy and pacing the floor with frustration. How stupid could she have been? Did she really think that he would react differently to the news about a baby? What was she going to do?

Rico was in shock as he looked at the phone in his hand. A baby was the last thing he needed to be concerned with and especially from someone he barely knew. As much as he had dreamed of one day being a father, he somehow knew that it would be with Sabrina.

As he sat replaying the conversation with Kendra over again in his head, he was distracted by the vibrating cellphone in his hand. Looking down at the caller ID, it was Alana. Shit. He thought to himself. He'd been so caught up with Sabrina he hadn't even considered the fact that Alana may have seen all the commotion played out in the news. He wasn't ready to deal with her, although he knew he had to end it; and soon he would need to be more strategic with her since she was a student at his place of employment. He sent the call to voicemail.

"Hey, it's Rico, I can't come to the phone right now. Leave me a message, after the beep." The voicemail seemed quick and cold.

"Hey Rico, it's me Alana. I have been trying to call you for a few days now and haven't been able to catch you. I hope everything is OK with you. Please call me when you get a chance. I am in Atlanta for the weekend but will be back in New York on Monday. My brother was in a car accident, and I needed to come home to check on him. Well, OK, I guess I will hear from you later. Bye."

Alana was disappointed that Rico didn't answer. She hadn't spoken with him in nearly a week, and she really wanted to talk to him about the attempted murder charge allegations surrounding him and his wife. She also needed to break the news to him about the baby. What would that conversation be like? Hell, how was she going to tell her family and when?

Rico saw the voicemail light indicated on the phone. He decided to listen to the message later. He needed to figure out how to handle this situation with Kendra. How did he get himself in this predicament? A baby! Really? That would destroy Sabrina. He had to end these extra-marital affairs. He loved his wife and for the first time in a long time realized he can't live without her.

He decided he would call it a night. He needed to be at the courthouse in the morning for Sabrina's appearance before the judge. He managed to secure an attorney that one of his students referred and prayed the man was good enough to at least secure a bond for Sabrina. He just couldn't bear the thought of her having to sleep night after night in a cold, hard jail cell. He laid down thinking…." I've got to fix this."

Chapter 12

Tyrone stopped on the way home to buy a bouquet of roses for Felicia. They hadn't really talked in the past two days, and he felt it was time to bury the hatchet. He had no intentions on hurting his wife or making her feel as if she wasn't the most important person in his life. He and Sherita had been through so much in their lifetime together that there were times over the past few years that gentle reminders presented themselves regarding their relationship. As he came through the garage door in the kitchen, he could hear the TV on in the family room. At quick glance he could see Felicia posted up on the sofa with her back to him pretending not to hear him coming in the door.

He walked up behind her.

"Hey babe, these are for you," he said as he leaned across the back of the couch presenting the beautiful flowers and kissing her on her left cheek.

She turned and gazed at him with amazement. She loved him so much, she found it difficult to stay angry with him for long periods of time.

"Thanks," she said gently taking them in her hands.

Tyrone came and sat next to his wife and put his arms around her pulling her into him for a hug.

"Hun, listen, about the other day at the hospital. Sherita and I have always had this cosmic connection to one another since we were in college. At times over the years, I hated her, but even more, for a while, she really was my best friend. I know that this all probably seems shallow and selfish, but trust me, there is nothing for you to be worried about where Sherita and I are concerned.

We love our kids and we have managed to figure out this maze of feelings since our divorce that has helped us to be better parents together." "Believe me," he said as he pulled her face toward his. "I love you and there is nothing that will change that. "I hope that we can discuss this if you want and truly put it all behind us and move on to where we all can be comfortable being in the same room together. I am not making an excuse for what you saw and I am certainly not dismissing how you must've felt, but I promise you it wasn't anything to worry about."

Felicia sat in silence looking at her husband as he poured out his heart to her.
Tyrone was a proud man who truly loved his family. Divorce for him was difficult and it took years for him to totally feel free enough to open his heart to love and trust again. Meeting Felicia changed his life, and he didn't want to ruin that feeling.

"Ty, sometimes I feel like I am in competition with her. I mean, she is your first wife and the mother of your children. She bares all the history with you and that is something I can never compete with," Felicia said with tears forming in her eyes.

"No, honey," he attempted to comfort her.

"Yes. I hear what you're saying, and I want to believe in my heart of hearts that it is true, but I promise there are times when I am not so sure," she confessed.

"Baby, listen to me. Don't you question your role in my life. Now, Sherita is a lot of things, but she is not the type of woman who would intentionally try to come in between me and my relationship.

She is happy for me and for us, and she wants to see us be a great couple. This is just a bump in the road that you and I didn't prepare for.

The past few years have been tough on all of us, and unfortunately my ex-wife and my kids were at the center of it all. But again, I promise you, it will be different."

Tyrone gently kissed Felicia's face on all sides. She reciprocated, and within seconds responded aggressively. She slowly turned and straddled her husband on the sofa kissing him impetuously. Tyrone stroked his wife's back and neck as he allowed his hands to touch every area of her body. He reversed their positioning and was lying on top of her kissing her with great anticipation. It had been weeks since they'd made love to one another, and he desperately wanted to reconnect.

"Oh, the joys of being in a house with no interruptions," he thought to himself as he gently planted kisses along her inner thigh.

Felicia responded willingly with confirming moans and body gestures. They were engrossed in one another, ready to explode and enjoy the intensity of love that had been bottled up inside for weeks. Felicia pulled Tyrone's shirt over his head as he quickly unhooked the clasps on her bra.

"Oh Ty, I love you so much," she said in between passionate kisses.

"I love you, too, Sher," he froze immediately, and the room stood still.

Chapter 13

Alana had one more day before heading back to New York. Josh seemed to be getting back to normal and doing pretty good. He still didn't want to see or talk to Tracy. Today was his first day back at work, and with everyone out of the house, Alana decided she would visit the walk-in clinic down the street to finally confirm her suspicions of being pregnant. She couldn't go to their family doctor as that would be a dead giveaway to her mom. Just as she was turning off the television to leave, the doorbell rang.

"Who is it?"

"Maggie's flower shop, I have a delivery here for a Sherita Coleman," the muffled voice shouted through the door.

Alana cracked the door to get a better view and saw that it was, in fact, a delivery person with an amazing arrangement of pink and white roses. She signed for them smiling gently as she placed them on the kitchen table for her mom to see when she got home.

"Kroy is such a good guy," she thought to herself. Assuming the flowers were from her stepfather.

She grabbed her keys and headed out the door.

Sitting in the small waiting area of the walk-in clinic, Alana tried to occupy her mind. She glanced at the small TV posted on the wall that was tuned to CNN. She noticed a headline regarding a New Jersey housewife being indicted on charges of attempting to murder her cheating husband. Then, she saw flashes of a woman's mug shot and a staff photo of Rico appear on the screen.

"Coleman," the nurse called.

"Um, that's me," she said softly as she stood to follow the small-framed woman to the back.

"Honey, I need you to stand on the scale. And when you're done, please step in the bathroom on the right and provide me with a urine sample."

Alana did as she was told. Feeling faint and sick to her stomach, she desperately prayed that her instincts were not true. After waiting in the small room for what seemed like hours, a doctor appeared.

"Hello Ms. Coleman. I am Doctor Tan, and I will be examining you today. First, let me start by saying congratulations to you. It appears as though you are going to have a baby."

Visibly upset at the news, Alana burst into tears. Crying uncontrollably, she wasn't sure what she should do or how she should handle the information.

"Now, now Ms. Coleman, it is alright. Being pregnant is oftentimes a shock to many women, but I assure you it is not the end of the world," Dr. Tan attempted to comfort Alana as best he could.
"Are you sure?" she asked with tears still flowing.

"I'm afraid so. I take it this was not a planned pregnancy?" he asked with empathy.

"My parents are going to kill me," she said in distress. "How could I be so stupid to let something like this happen? I've got one more year to graduate from NYU and now this! My life is ruined," Alana was hysterical.

"Ms. Coleman, sit down for a minute and just breathe. Come on now. Talk to me for a minute, exactly why do you think your life is over? I mean, you appear to be a relatively responsible young woman, who just so happens to be at a different crossroad in life than what you expected. Now, what about the baby's father? Is he able to support the two of you?" Dr. Tan was concerned.

"Umm, yes. I mean, no. I mean, hell I don't know what the 'baby's father' will do!" Alana screamed as she formed quotation marks in the air with her hands.

"You see Dr. Sun or Tan or whatever the hell your name is, that is exactly why looks can be deceiving. I actually am NOT a responsible young woman, seeing as how I have managed to get knocked up by my college professor who, not only is married, but his wife just got indicted on attempted murder charges TODAY for trying to kill his ass! "So, NO, I don't know what the 'FATHER' will do. He doesn't even know I'm PREGNANT!"

"Oh dear," were the only words Dr. Tan could utter in disbelief.

An uncomfortable silence ensued as Alana sobbed. In an effort to console her again, Dr. Tan spoke first.

"Well, you're right. It appears as though you've gotten yourself into a bit of a pickle. However, trust me, it will all work itself out," he said as he patted her soothingly on the knee.

"So, with that being said, let's check you out and get a full look at you and determine exactly how long in the process you are, talk about healthy habits and get you started on this journey. Shall we?"

With a deep sigh, Alana laid back on the cold examining table with a myriad of thoughts running through her head. She had no idea what Dr. Tan was saying because, at that moment, she'd tuned him out.

What was she going to do?

After 30 minutes the exam was over. Alana waited patiently for Dr. Tan to return to the room after she finished putting her clothes back on.

Knock knock...

"Good. You're all dressed. So, from the looks of it, I would say you are about 10 or 11 weeks along, so coming up on the end of your first trimester. I would highly encourage you to start now in seeing your OB/GYN physician so that he or she can continue to monitor your progress and ensure that all the necessary steps and testing takes place during the appointed times.
I am giving you a sample pack of prenatal vitamins to start with, but again be sure to see your physician as soon as possible as they may recommend something different based upon your health history.

"Please be sure to eat at least three meals a day and incorporate some level of exercise daily to help with the pending changes that may occur.

Try to stay away from fried foods, foods high in sodium and sugar as they are not good for you or your unborn child. It is too early to determine the sex of your baby, but around your 15th or 16th week, you should be able to find out that information should you wish to know it.

"Lastly, young lady, please know that everything will work itself out. I suggest you start by having a discussion with the father and then with your family to help you get through this process. Now, do you have any questions?" he asked politely.

"No. Thank you."

"Well then, you can make your payment up front on your way out. Please feel free to stop by anytime you need anything, our office is open Monday through Sunday from 7:00 a.m. to 10:00 p.m.," he said as he extended a handshake to Alana.

Alana was in a daze as she drove back to the house. She pulled over into a vacant parking lot to gather herself together before she got home. She wasn't ready to see anybody and have them know instantly that something was wrong. She decided to try Rico on his cell. Now was as good a time as any to break the news to him.

"Yeah!" he answered abruptly.

"Well, hello to you, too," she replied sarcastically.

"I'm sorry. I've got a lot going on right now. What's up?"

"Umm, is everything OK? I saw the news earlier, what is going on?" she asked.

"Well, if you saw the news, then you pretty much know what's going on. So why would you ask such a dumb-ass question?"

"Hey! Listen, I am not the enemy here, so you need to tone it down a bit."

"Yeah, I guess. Listen, Lan, we need to talk," he jumped right in.

"Yeah, I know. That's why I'm calling you. Rico… I'm pregnant."

"What? You, too?" Rico was in shock. "What the hell else could go wrong in my life," he screamed as he looked up toward the sky in disbelief.

"Wait a minute, what do you mean, you, too?" Alana questioned. "Is there something you need to share with me Rico other than the real reason why your wife is in county lockup on attempted murder charges for trying to bury yo' ass?"

"Look, I don't have time for this. Right now, I have got to work all of this out between me and Sabrina and get us out of this mess. Honestly, a baby is the last thing on my mind. When are you returning to New York? Maybe I can meet you and give you a couple hundred dollars or sumthin' to get it taken care of, but that's as much as I can commit to right now," his words were cold and distant.

"Are you freaking kidding me right now? Did you just offer to give me money for an abortion? You SON-OF-A-BITCH!"

"Yeah, well that's all I got," and he hung up the phone.

In shock and infuriated, Alana was once again in tears. This time, tears of outrage and anger. She sat in her car literally screaming at the top of her lungs and honking the horn furiously in an attempt to blow off steam. After a few minutes of rage, she calmed down and sat numb gazing out the window. This all seemed like a bad nightmare that she wanted to wake up from. She decided to call Bella.

"Hello," a strange voice answered on the other end.

"I'm sorry, I must've dialed the wrong number," Alana replied politely.

"Who'd you like to speak with," the voice asked again.

"Is this Bella's phone?"

"Yes, it is. Who's calling?"

"This is Alana. Is Bella available?"

"Oh, Ah-laan-aah. Well, if it isn't little miss goody-two-shoes," Hustle said in a sinister tone.

"Oh, if it isn't the carpet muncher. Look, put Bella on the phone, I don't have time to play games with you, Hustle."

"Games? Who's playing games? I just answered my sweetie's phone. More than I can say for you right now. Heard you were picking out a black dress."

"Look, is Bella there or not?"

"Not, but I might tell her you called. Or I might not, but I am sure before the night is over, WE will hear from you sooner rather than later," Hustle said defiantly.

"What the hell does that mean? You know what? Nevermind, you trippin'. Just tell Bella I called."

Alana hung up the phone. She didn't have time to play head games with Hustle. That chick was crazy and out of control, and she was the last person Alana would let add more stress to her day. She checked her rearview mirror to make sure she didn't look like she'd been crying all day. Alana decided to head home and lay down before dinner with the family.

As she pulled into the driveway, she noticed that only Josh's car was home, so hopefully she could head straight to her room without any issues. Josh was on the sofa watching sports when Alana walked in the room.

"Hey sis. You good?" he asked without looking away from the TV.

"Yeah. I'm good," she replied as she headed down the hall to her room. She noticed the flowers were still where she left them earlier.

"Hey Josh, has Mom not been home?" she yelled down the hall.

"Nah, I don't think so. I just got in from work and nobody was here. I think she and Kroy went looking at buildings or something."

"Buildings?"

"Yeah, dude is thinking 'bout opening up an art gallery here in Atlanta or something like that. You know I don't know the full scope, I just listen from time-to-time," he said rambling.

"Hmph," she replied.

Alana closed the door to her room and laid down across the bed on her back. Without thinking of it, she gently rubbed her stomach. This entire day had been troubling. With one year left of school, how would she be able to graduate with a baby? She was planning on spending the summer in Trinidad next year doing an internship with a friend of Kroy's family business. So much for that idea! She needed to come up with a plan. When would she tell her mom? What would her dad have to say? They are going to be devastated. In that instance, she knew who she could call for advice, Aunt Kendra.

Kendra answered the phone after the third ring. She was trying to get herself together emotionally after having been glued to the television all morning. She was in shock at the news reports from New Jersey involving Rico. No wonder he'd been acting strange. His ass is married!

"Hello," Kendra answered calmly.

"Um, hey Aunt Kendra, it's me, Alana. Are you busy?"

"Hey Lan, sweetie. I umm. No, I'm not busy, what's up? Is everything OK?"

"Well, not quite. I need to talk to you about something."

Putting the TV on mute, Kendra could sense the nervousness in Alana's voice.

"Honey, what's wrong?"

"Well…"

Just as Alana was about to share her story, there was a knock on her bedroom door. It was Sherita.

"Lan, sweetie. You asleep?"

"Hold on, Aunt Kendra."

"No, Mom, I'll be right out."

"OK. Is everything alright?" Sherita asked.

"Yeah, I'm fine. I'm on the phone."

"Well, don't be too long. I want you to help me get dinner started," Sherita yelled through the closed door.

"OK. I'm coming. …Hello?"

"Yeah, I'm here. Sweetie, you want to give me a call back a little later. Sounds like your mom needs you," Kendra said with concern.

"OK, I'll call you after dinner; if that's OK?"

Kendra's other line clicked while she was talking to Alana. Looking at the caller ID she could see it was Sherita.

"OK, honey, this is your mom on the other line, let me click over and talk to her. Call me later."

"OK. Thanks Aunt Kendra."

"Hello," Kendra answered like nothing was wrong.

"Girl, what'chu doin? What took you so long to answer the phone? Why didn't you call me back the other night?" Sherita playfully asked one question after the other.

"Well damn, the last time I checked my Momma was in Adamsville," Kendra replied sharply.

"Yeah, and if she knew you weren't calling me back like you suppose to, she would be asking these same questions!"

The two burst into laughter. Sherita and Kendra had a way of reminding one another of their teenage days as girls. The sense of balance between the two was a unique and strong bond.

"Chile, what is going on with you over there? How was your day?" Sherita asked with a smile on her face.

"It's been a long day, Sher. But I am just glad it is over. I haven't been myself lately, you know?"

"Tell me about it. I wasn't gonna say anything, but I noticed you've been a bit distant over the past few weeks. What's going on? Is there something you want to talk about?"

"Well, I guess I'm gonna have to tell it to you sooner or later," Kendra said with a sigh.

"What? What are you talking about? Is something wrong Kendra?"

Kendra's eyes filled with tears as she struggled to control the flutter in her voice. The last thing she wanted was to panic Sherita and have her at her doorstep dressed in black with her hair pulled back and ready to bust somebody's windows out of their car.

Just as Kendra was about to reveal her secret, she noticed on the news that they were discussing Rico's case again. She quickly un-muted the TV to hear what they were saying.

"Kendra, girl, what are you doing?"

"Shhh, hold on a minute, Sher. I'm trying to hear something on television."

"Girl, are you watching CNN? That story about that chick who tried to kill her cheating husband is crazy! People done lost they minds. I tell you, it's just not worth it. She should've just left his lying ass and moved on with her life," Sherita voiced her strong opinion on the case.

Hearing every word her friend was saying, Kendra felt nervous.

How would she tell Sherita that the lying, cheating, scumbag of a husband who narrowly beat death at the hands of his scorned wife just so happens to be the father of her unborn child; and, oh by the way, she's the low life he's been cheating with; although she didn't know the asshole was married.

"Sher, I need to call you back, my mom is on the other line," Kendra lied as she immediately hung up the phone.

"Huh? Kendra!" Sherita was confused. Kendra has really been acting strange lately, but what else was new? The past few years have proven to be unusual in day-to-day life.

Alana walked into the kitchen just as her mom was turning away from the news report out of New Jersey. She was nervous. She noticed the flowers on the table were still untouched.

"Hey mom, what's for dinner?" Alana asked, trying to act normal.

Just as she sat down at the table, Kroy walked in the kitchen and approached Sherita from the back and provided a loving embrace and quick kiss on the cheek.

"Mi' Amore," he said as he kissed her.

"Hey babe. How was your day?" Sherita asked with a smile.

"Hey Lan. How are you today?" Kroy asked acknowledging Alana's presence in the room.

"Hey. I'm good. Thank you," she replied.

"Wow, nice flowers, what's the occasion?" Kroy asked.

"Oh, I don't know. They were here when I got home. I assumed they were Alana's."

"Ah, No! Mom they are for you. They came this morning. I figured Kroy was up to his old tricks again and sending his "Mi' Amore" flowers," Alana said with a giggle and googly eyes.

"For me? Really? Hun, did you send these earlier today?" Sherita was confused.

Throwing his hands in the air as if to indicate surrender, Kroy said: "Wasn't me."

While the three were trying to determine where the flowers came from, Josh walks in.

"Oh my Gosh, just read the card already! Y'all act like it's a mystery gift and that they're going to explode," Josh said as he snatched the card from the stick inside the bouquet.

Fluffy blankets and rosy cheeks are the things that are anticipated for 48 weeks. So, with 10 toes and 10 fingers the love that is garnered continues to linger. The first grandchild is always the best, they steal your heart from all the rest. So, as you celebrate with this joyous rhyme, CONGRATULATIONS on becoming a grandparent for the very first time!
Congratulations Mrs. Coleman to you and Alana!

Josh, mouth agape, stared blankly at the card. Everyone in the room was speechless as they all turned to look at Alana.

"What the hell is that, Josh?" Alana asked as she jumped up and snatched the card from her brother's hand.

"Hey, I just read what was on the card."

"Alana, what is going on?" Sherita was confused.

"Lan, are you pregnant?" Kroy asked calmly.

Alana felt faint. What was going on? Who sent this to her mom? Who knew? Looking around the room aimlessly, she knew she needed to respond.

"Mom, I'm so sorry," she stated as she looked into her mother's questioning eyes.

"Lan, what's going on? You need to start talking young lady and you need to do it fast," Sherita was pissed.

"I'm pregnant," she said with tears in her eyes.

"PREGNANT?" Josh yelled. "By who? How could you let this happen, Lan? Are you serious right now?"

"Alana Rene' Coleman, are you telling me that you are one year away from graduating from New York University with a degree in Journalism, with a pending job already lined up in the Port of Spain for next summer and you are now PREGNANT?" Sherita questioned as calmly as she could.

"OK, OK, let's everyone calm down for a bit and give her an opportunity to explain," Kroy attempted to be the voice of reason.

"I really don't have an explanation. I'm pregnant. I was irresponsible and didn't think through my actions. None of them," she said with her head hung low in embarrassment.

"Lan, who is the father of this baby? Does he know you're pregnant? Is he a student as well? Sweetheart, have you thought through any of this?" Sherita had what felt like a million and one questions.

"He knows I'm pregnant. He's not a student."

"Well, who is he? Some random dude," Josh wanted a better response than what he was getting.

"Shut-up Josh! This isn't any of your business anyway," Alana lashed back.

"Really? You're telling me to shut up? Lan, you're an idiot!"

"Hey, that's enough! Josh, sit yo' ass down and shut the hell up," Sherita yelled.

"I'm outta here," Josh left and headed to his room.

"Mi' Amore, I'm gonna let you two talk in private," Kroy said as he kissed Sherita's forehead and headed in the family room.

Sherita and Alana sat silently across from one another. Sherita was full of mixed emotions surrounding this shocking news. She knew that Alana was deeply saddened by her actions and needed support at this time to help figure out what to do next. Still, she was very upset with her daughter.

She didn't envision babies for a few more years to come and had hoped that a wedding would precede children. Lord, how were they going to tell Tyrone?

Chapter 14

Bella's hands were full of grocery bags as she made it up the 3 flights of stairs to her apartment. She was pissed she left out earlier and forgot her cellphone on the kitchen counter. As she made it to the top, she managed to free one of her hands to gently knock on the door.

"Yeah?!" Hustled yelled from the other side.

"Hey, it's me. Can you open up I can't reach my keys?"

Opening the door, Hustle immediately grabbed a couple of the bags from Bella's hands.

"Oh my gosh, Belle! Why didn't you tell me you were going grocery shopping? I could've come with you to help carry this stuff."

"Well, I got in there and realized I needed more than I thought and once I paid for everything noticed that I didn't have my cellphone to call, so I figured I would be OK."

"Miss Independent," Hustle replied.

"What's going on with you? What are you up to?"

"Oh, not much. Just been watching the news all day. Yo' that shit is crazy with that Professor dude from your school, right? Isn't he the one that ol' girl is creepin' with?"

"Hustle, what are you talking about?"

"Ol' girl. Your friend Alana. The pregnant chick, isn't that the dude she been messin' 'round with?"

"Hustle, how do you know that?"

"What do you mean? How do I know that? Is it some sort of secret or something? Hell, y'all was talking 'bout it last week like it was public knowledge and shit."

"Umph, public knowledge, huh? Hustle, that is none of your business, so please stay out of it. Alana is a really good friend to me, and I already feel bad with all that she is having to deal with. I don't need her thinking she doesn't have my support."

"Well, why the hell would she need your support, Bella? What can you do for her? She is the one sleeping with a married man and obviously not smart enough not to get knocked up. Or wait, maybe she did it intentionally?"

"HUSTLE! You are being ridiculous! You don't even know her and besides, Alana would never do anything like that."

"Yeah, well, I call it like I see it."

Hustle sat down on the sofa in front of the television. Bella started putting the groceries up in the kitchen. She picked up her cell phone off the counter and noticed Alana had called. Strangely enough, it said the call lasted 4.5 minutes.

"Hey, did Alana call me today?"

"Oh, yeah. She did. She sounded upset about something. I told her you weren't here. Don't worry, I'm sure she will be calling back sooner rather than later."

"What does that mean?"

"Nothing. Nothing at all," she said defiantly. "By the way Belle, what's for dinner?"

Bella was a bit uneasy with Hustle's sarcastic demeanor. She'd known her all her life and knew the types of craziness she could scheme up when she felt threatened by someone. She knew that Hustle felt some kind of way about Alana and would do any and everything she could to drive a wedge between them. Although she loved her very much, she was growing weary of Hustle's jealous ways. Bella took her phone, went to the bedroom and closed the door behind her. She needed to check on Alana. There was a lot going on and she knew that she was probably freaking out.

Alana's phone went straight to voicemail.

"Hey Lan, it's me Bella. Just got home and saw where you called earlier. I left my phone on the table this morning, so I apologize for not being available. OK, well, call me back. Just wanted to check on you to make sure you're good."

As Bella sat on the side of the bed, she noticed a piece of paper on the nightstand that had a phone number for Maggie's flower shop in Atlanta. Before she could say anything about the note, Hustle entered the room. She pushed Bella back on the bed climbed on top of her and started kissing her profusely.

Not given an opportunity to reject her lover's advances, Bella quickly gave in to her growing level of emotions. Hustle was in complete control. Within minutes, she'd managed to undress Bella from the waist down and proceeded to please her in ways that were overwhelming.

As the two made love, their activities lasted late into the night. As Hustle lay asleep across Bella's chest, she stared up at the ceiling through the darkness. Startled by the buzzing vibration of her cellphone, Bella noticed in the caller ID that it was Alana. She clicked the on button.
"Hey Lan. Hold on," she said whispering.

Looking at the clock, it was nearly 2:00 a.m. She knew Hustle was out like a light and gently eased herself from up under her lover's restless body. Once free, she grabbed a pair of boxer shorts off the floor and headed to the bathroom. Closing the door, she sat down on the side of the tub.

"Lan, you there?"

"Yeah. I'm here. Belle, sorry for calling so late, but I just needed someone to talk to."

"No. No, sweetie. You don't have to apologize. I am always here for you no matter what time it is. How you holding up?"

"Well, I went to the walk-in clinic today."

"And?"

"And I'm pregnant."

"Oh no. Lan, I am so sorry. Are you alright?"

"No. This has been the worst day of my life."

"What happened? Did you tell your folks?"

"Hmph, seems as though someone felt it necessary to share the news for me."

"Huh? What do mean?"

"Somebody sent my mom a bouquet of flowers congratulating her on becoming a first-time grandmother. It was just so bizarre that I can't even wrap my head around where they came from or who?"

Bella was instantly infuriated. She immediately put two and two together realizing what Hustle had done. This had her name written all over it.

"Lan, are you serious? What'd your mother say?"

"What do you think? It was a shouting match with her and my brother for about 30 minutes."

"Have you told your dad?"

"No. Not yet. My mom tried to call him to ask him to come over to tell him together but he didn't answer the phone. He is supposed to be taking me to the airport in the morning to come back to New York, so I guess I will tell him then."

"What about Rico? Any word from him?"

"That asshole. When I talked to him and told him I was pregnant, he told me he didn't have time to deal with it and that his focus right now was him and his wife. He offered to give me a couple hundred dollars to 'take care of it'," she said making quotation gestures with her hands.

"What!? Lan, are you serious?"

"Yeah."

"What an asshole! His wife should've shot his fucking penis off!" Bella was angry.

"I know right. Well, I guess once I have this discussion with my dad we will see if I even live to tell the story."

"Oh boy. I bet. So, what'd the doctor say?"

"I'm between 8 and 10 weeks, I think. I have to schedule an appointment with an OB/GYN to have an ultrasound done for a more confirming timeframe. He told me to eat three meals a day, exercise and not to worry."

"He sounds like a real gem."

"Yeah, I think I freaked him out when I started screaming and crying hysterically."

"Oh lord, Lan. You didn't show out on the man, did you?" Bella asked with a chuckle.

"If only you knew. I'm sure he couldn't wait to get my ass up out of that exam room. It's funny now."

"Well, look at it this way. In the event that your dad lets you live tomorrow, there is a bright side."

"Gee, really? And what would that bright side be?"

"Girl, I am going to be an AUNTIE!" she said with excitement in her voice.

"Shut the hell up, Bella! Who needs all that damn excitement in their life right now?"

"Well get used to it, because I am."

"Lord, what am I gonna do?"

"Be a great Mom. That's what you are going to do and I will be here every step of the way. I promise."

"Thanks Belle. I love you."

"I love you, too, chica. Call me when you get back to New York tomorrow."

"I will. Goodnight."

"Goodnight."

Bella went into the kitchen and got a cold bottle of water out the refrigerator and headed back in the bedroom. She opened the bottle and poured it all on Hustle's sleeping head. Startled, Hustle thought she was drowning. She jumped up.

"WHAT THE HELL ARE YOU DOING BELLA?" she screamed.

Flipping on the overhead light, Bella stood over the bed with the note from the nightstand displaying "Maggie's Flower Shop".

"Hmm, seems that question should be 'what the hell have YOU done, Hustle'?"

Smiling slyly, Hustle erupted into loud laughter while falling back on the bed, kicking and giggling with glee.

"HUSTLE! What is your problem? What did you do?" Bella was furious.

"Who me? I only sent my well-wishes to a family that is about to welcome life into this wonderful world we live in. Is that so wrong, Belle?"

"Hustle, I can't believe you. Why would you do something so stupid? I told you. Alana is my friend, and you are out of order for getting in her business. Why would you do something so mean and hateful?"

"Listen, that little bitch deserved it. Besides, maybe now that she has her own life to get in order, she can stay the hell out of ours."

"What are you talking about? She isn't in our life? She is the only person that we've ever told about our relationship who off the rip was nothing but supportive. So I am just a tad bit confused at your level of jealousy toward her? She hasn't done anything to you or to me!"

"Yeah well, I don't like her. And I don't like you hanging around her."

"Well, you not liking Alana is your problem. And as far as me not hanging around her, well, that will be your problem, too. As a matter of fact, ever since you've been in New York, Hustle you've been nothing but added stress in my life. I think it's time for you to go back to California. I've got one more year of school to get through and the last thing I need in my life is drama from you being jealous of my life and my friends. I will book you a plane ticket in the morning. I need you gone by tomorrow night."

Bella was serious. She grabbed a blanket out the closet and headed for the sofa out front. As much as she loved Hustle, she'd realized for a long time that this relationship was toxic.

Speechless, Hustle was in shock as she watched Bella walk out of the room. Was she really serious? Was Bella breaking up with her?

That bitch Alana is gonna pay...she thought to herself as she laid back down.

Chapter 15

Tyrone couldn't sleep. He noticed he had several missed calls from Sherita on his cellphone but decided it was best to put some space between the two of them for a while.

He loved Felicia and couldn't for the life of him understand why all of a sudden, he was experiencing this wave of emotions for his ex-wife. He and Sherita had long since put their feelings for one another behind them. Josh and Alana were his only priority where that relationship was concerned.

As he scrolled through the phone, he noticed several missed calls from Josh and Alana as well.

What is going on over there? He thought to himself.

Looking at the clock it was nearly 2:30 in the morning. He needed to try and get some sleep; he'd have to be up soon to take Alana to the airport. As he turned off the lights in the kitchen, the phone rang. It was Alana.

"Sweetie is everything OK?" he asked immediately concerned with the time his daughter was calling.

"Hey daddy. Are you sleeping?"

"Don't I wish? Been having a little difficulty making that happen the past couple of days. What's going on baby girl? Why are you still up at this hour?"

"Well, Daddy... I have something I need to tell you. We tried calling you earlier, but you didn't answer, and I just couldn't go to sleep without at least talking to you about this," Alana was scared.

"Lan, what's going on? Is your brother, OK?"

"Hmph? Yes, I mean, yeah Daddy, everything is OK with Josh. He's fine."

"Did something happen with your mom?" Tyrone was getting agitated.

Alana felt tears streaming down her face. She was terribly nervous.

"Daddy... I'm pregnant," she blurted it out so fast that she felt herself wincing as if she anticipated her dad raising his hand to hit her.

"You're what?"

"I'm pregnant, Daddy."

"Wait, wait, wait...if I am hearing you correctly. It is 2:35 in the morning and you just called my phone and told me that you are pregnant?" Tyrone was numb. "Now what exactly am I supposed to do with that information, Alana?"

"Daddy, I'm sorry."

"SORRY? SORRY!

I am paying close to a hundred thousand dollars a year for you to go to live in New York, go to NYU to get an education with ONE YEAR left to graduate and your only statement following you telling me "you're pregnant" is that "YOU'RE SORRY"?

Girl, you better be damn glad you chose to tell me about this shit over the phone, cause if I were face-to-face with you I would choke every dime of my money outta yo' ass right now!"

"DADDY!" Alana screamed through her tears.

"Daddy WHAT Alana? How the hell are you going to take care of a baby? Who is the father? What is he planning on doing? Does he work? Can he support you?" Tyrone was yelling one question after the other.

Hearing all the commotion, Felicia came running into the kitchen.

"Tyrone, what is going on?" she said with a look of confusion on her face.

"Alana, I am not about to deal with this shit. You and your mother are going to have to figure this out on your own. You hear me? I am NOT dealing with this bullshit!" he screamed as he hung up the phone.

Tyrone was furious. He slung the cellphone across the room and turned around and punched a hole in the wall. He snatched his keys off the counter and stormed out the back door.

"TYRONE! TYRONE!" Felicia yelled after her husband who wasn't hearing anything she was saying as he slammed the door.

Alana sat on the floor of her room crying uncontrollably as she held the phone in her hands.

Josh, Sherita and Kroy all appeared at her bedroom door as they heard her crying out loud and wasn't sure what was going on?

"Alana, honey, what happened?" Sherita asked with concern seeing her daughter in tears on the floor.
"Hmph, looks like she called Dad," Josh said sarcastically as he turned and went back to his room.

Looking at Kroy, Sherita didn't know what to do. Kroy shook his head and rubbed his chin with his hand in disbelief. He turned and followed Josh down the hall leaving Sherita standing in the door to Alana's room.

Kneeling on the floor in front of her daughter, Sherita pulled Alana into her chest and just started to rock her back and forth. There were no words that she could offer to help her feel better about the encounter with her dad. Tyrone loved his kids and they loved him. He had the highest level of expectations for them and when they disappointed him, they felt every bit of anger he had regarding it. Sherita knew this news would devastate Ty. Lord, how would they move past the events of the week?

Kroy quietly approached the door to hand Sherita her cellphone. It was Felicia.

"Hello," Sherita answered the phone.

"Do you and your children intentionally create drama to keep my husband actively engaged in your lives?" Felicia asked in a cynical manner.

"Hello? Felicia?" Sherita had to catch the voice on the other end of the phone.

"Listen, I am sorry that you can't seem to keep your children under control, but, at this point, you all need to stop calling Tyrone for every little thing that goes wrong in your household. I am SICK of it and it will stop now!" Felicia insisted.

"Chile, I know good and damn well you are not on my phone threatening me about my children and THEIR father who happens to be married to your crazy ass? And for your information, if we choose to have drama from now until the end of time, nothing is going to EVER stop Tyrone from making sure that HIS children are OK. So, I suggest, you get a grip and get it together because WE ain't going nowhere."

"See, that right there is the problem MRS. LABEAUF! YOU are not a part of that 'we' any longer. Therefore, you shouldn't even be in the midst of what happens between Tyrone and his children."

"Well, seeing as how you have NO children to relate to, I don't expect you to ever understand. Now I have tried to be nice to you, embrace you and even help make you a part of this family. But you have come at me the wrong way one too many times, and my patience with you is running short. So, hear me clearly when I say to you, I suggest you figure out how to be a loving and supportive wife where my kids are concerned with their dad or else this life you live now will become a nightmare," Sherita meant business.

"Are you threatening me?"

"No ma'am. Not at all. You see, I don't make threats, I make promises. And if you mess with my kids, it's gonna take more than Tyrone Coleman to keep me off yo' ass. So, thank you Felicia, for your 3:00 a.m. call of concern.

We appreciate your level of support. Please have my EX-husband call us when he calms down."

Sherita hung up the phone. She hadn't realized that she was breathing heavy and sweating. The nerve of Felicia calling her house at 3 in the morning talking crazy! Clearly, she don't know what or who she is dealing with.

The energy of the evening had taken a toll on Sherita. In the midst of her conversation with Felicia, she had nearly paced a hole in the floor in the hallway. Her head had started to hurt. Sherita sat down at the kitchen table massaging her throbbing temples.

This whole family needs to go to church, she thought to herself.

Alana sobbed silently as she sat on the floor thinking of the mess she'd caused. What could she do? How was she going to fix this? She was exhausted both mentally and physically. She finally drug herself up off the floor and laid down.

This had been the craziest day of her life. How did she get herself into this mess? She couldn't help but think about her dad and how disappointed he sounded over the phone. Would he ever forgive her? Could she ever forgive herself?

Her mind was racing. She really needed to get some sleep to catch her flight in the morning back to New York. She hated herself, but she was beginning to hate Rico even more.

Although the news was out to her family about the pregnancy, she would still have to deal with the fact that it was a result of an inappropriate relationship with a married professor who just so happens to be on national news for his estranged wife trying to kill him. Whew…. this has got to be a nightmare!

Chapter 16

Rico paced out front of courtroom D for what felt like hours. It was a few minutes before court opened and he wanted to be inside on the front row for Sabrina's arraignment hearing. He'd managed to secure a criminal defense attorney and hoped that she would be granted bail today and be allowed to come home. This entire incident had been unbelievable and to think not only was his wife behind bars for attempted murder, but both of the women he'd been having extramarital affairs with were claiming to be pregnant. As he began to enter the courtroom, he noticed Sabrina's mom and cousin getting off the elevator.

"Good morning, Ms. Clara. Thank you so much for coming," Rico said as he greeted his mother-in-law.

"Yeah, well, let's be clear, I am not here for you. It's because of your actions that my baby is even in this mess."

Clara was never a fan of Rico, and this episode proved her suspicions about him all along.

As the three entered the courtroom, they saw an officer escort Sabrina in from a side door in handcuffs. She was wearing the blue dress that Rico had dropped off at the station for her Friday. She looked tired, old, and scared. The attorney leaned over and whispered something in her ear and shortly thereafter she looked back and gave a forced smile to her mother and her cousin. She never made eye contact with Rico.

"All rise. The Honorable Judge Helen Middleton is presiding," the bailiff announced. "Court is now in session."

"You may be seated," Judge Middleton stated. "Good morning, everyone.

We have a very full docket today and therefore we will proceed accordingly. Looks like we are here for the arraignment hearing of Mrs. Sabrina Harris, is that correct?

"Yes, your honor," replied the prosecuting attorney.

Adjusting her glasses, Judge Middleton read the charges aloud.

"Mrs. Harris is being charged with 1 count of attempted murder, 1 count of unlicensed possession of a firearm, and 1 count of reckless conduct and endangerment. How does the defendant wish to plea?"

"Umm, your honor on the count of attempted murder my client pleads not guilty," Sabrina's attorney timidly chimed in, "the counts of unlicensed possession of a firearm and reckless conduct and endangerment, she pleads guilty."

"It appears, counselor, as if your client intentionally opened fire on her husband, and he was the only target. Was she not trying to kill him?"

"No ma'am, your honor, she was just trying to scare him."

"Scare him? I see. Well, bail is set at $500,000 and a court date to appear 30 days from today."

As the judge announced the enormous bail, shrieks erupted in the courtroom from Sabrina's mom and cousin as they cried loudly.

Sabrina sat calmly with tears streaming down her face. Where would she be able to come up with $50,000 for bond money?

"Your honor, may I address the court?" asked the defense attorney.

"Go ahead."

"Your honor, with all due respect, Mrs. Harris is a first-time offender. She's never been in trouble with the law before and she doesn't pose a flight risk. I'd like to ask for a more affordable bail."

"Well counselor, your client should have thought of that before she decided to 'scare' her husband. Let the court records reflect bail for the accused is set at $500,000. If she is not able to make bail, then Mrs. Harris shall remain in county lockup until her scheduled court appearance 30 days from today."

And with the stroke of a gavel, Sabrina could feel the deputy standing next to her encouraging her to stand and be handcuffed. Rico was in shock, he sat staring at his wife in disbelief. What were they going to do? He'd have to come up with the money some type of way. He couldn't allow Sabrina to spend any more time in jail.

"Oh! My Baby!" Clara cried out.

"Ms. Clara, it's going to be alright," Rico tried to soothe his mother-in-law.

"You son-of-a-bitch, don't you touch me! This is ALL your fault! Had you not been traipsing around town with whomever and wherever Sabrina wouldn't be in this mess! You are the devil walking!"

Sabrina's cousin grabbed her aunt's arm and led her out of the courtroom. Glaring back at a stunned Rico, the two women were visibly angry.

Rico sat on the bench outside of the courtroom for a few minutes just trying to process everything. He had to come up with this money and fast. Who did he know who could help him? His brother Russell, a known drug dealer would be the only person who could get his hands on that type of cash fast. He made the call.

"Hey Russell, man it's Rico, hit me back as soon as you get this message. It's an emergency."

Just as he hung up, the phone rang. It was Alana.

"Hey. It's me. I need to see you."

"Look, Alana, now is not a good time."

"Now is the best time or else you're going to have bigger problems than your wife in county lockup. Meet me at the bookstore at the corner of 125th and 12th streets in a half hour."

She hung up.

"Ugh! This is some BULLSHIT!" Rico screamed as he headed toward the elevator.

The last thing he needed was Alana causing more issues with the university. He swung by the bank on the way to the bookstore and took out $300 cash.

Alana waited near the window inside the coffee shop of the bookstore for Rico to arrive. She came straight there once her flight landed from Atlanta. Tyrone didn't show up to take her to the airport this morning and so her mom and Kroy

dropped her off early. She wondered if her dad would ever speak to her again. Sherita and Kroy tried their best to be supportive, but the long bouts of silence on the drive were grueling.

As she sipped on a cup of tea, she noticed Rico rounding the corner.

"Hello."

"What do you want Alana?" Rico didn't bother with any pleasantries.

"What do I want? I want you to acknowledge the fact that I am pregnant and that we need to talk about this. That is what I want," she said in a stern hushed voice.

"Yeah, well, as I mentioned to you on the phone, that is not a part of my plan at the moment. All I can offer you is money for an abortion; otherwise, I really don't care what you do," he said as he took the cash out of his pocket and placed it on the table.

"You really think you can just push me off with a few hundred dollars in cash? How dare you insult me that way?

My life is ruined as a result of all of this, and you expect to just walk away and not have any level of responsibility?"

"Responsibility? Is that what you're bringing up? Being responsible?

You didn't seem to care about that when you were screwing my brains out every chance you got. You knew from the beginning I was married. I never gave you any reason to believe that this would be more than just something to do."

"Something to do, huh? Well, this is going to be one time in your life that you wished you'd taken up a different hobby. Keep your money. You're gonna need it."

Alana had a look of fire in her eyes as she stood and headed for the door. Who the hell did Rico think he was; acting like this whole thing was her fault?

She headed uptown to her apartment. She felt nauseated and needed to lie down. Now that she knew exactly where Rico stood in this whole baby issue, she knew that it wouldn't be long before she would have to tell her mom the truth about who the father was. She decided to get some advice from Kendra to see if she could help her figure out the best way to break the news. Of everyone in her family, Aunt Kendra would be able to help it all make sense.

"Hey Aunt Kendra, it's me Lan – please give me a call when you get this message. I really need to talk to you."

Chapter 17

Kendra agreed to meet Sherita at a local brunch spot not far from her house. Although it was still early in the day, the two could use an establishment that served mimosas around the clock.

Kendra arrived early and, to kill time, perused the internet on her cellphone. Keeping track of the case in New York, she almost screamed out loud when, yet another photo of the cheating husband appeared on the screen. She was still in shock that this was Rico!

"Hey honey, how are you this morning? You, OK? You look like you've just seen a ghost?"

Sherita became concerned immediately as she took a seat across from her best friend of more than 20 years.

Kendra's face was pale, she felt sick to her stomach all of a sudden. She was at a loss for words as she gazed helplessly across at Sherita.

"Kendra? Honey, you're scaring me. What is going on? What are you looking at?"

Kendra took a deep breath and grabbed Sherita's hands across the table.

"Sher. I'm pregnant."

"What?" Sherita said in disbelief. "I mean, how? When? Who?"

Sherita and Kendra had been friends since high school and had always shared every aspect of each other's life.

She was confused at the thought that Kendra had been involved with someone so intimately and she had no idea. Had she really been that consumed in her own life and marriage to Kroy that she neglected to be the best friend she could be?

"I know, I know you've got a million questions and hopefully I have at least half of the answers."

"I'm listening."

"Excuse me ladies, are you ready to order?" The waitress interrupted.

"Large cup of coffee with low-fat milk and a bowl of sugar cubes and she'll have…. well, I guess she will have a glass of milk!" Sherita said sarcastically as she stared at Kendra from across the table, never once making eye-contact with the waitress.

"Sherita, I really need you right now. I know I should've told you earlier and I apologize, but I wasn't sure what to do or what I was going to do for that matter."

"Kendra, I am your friend! When have you EVER known what the hell to do and didn't call me to work through the logistics?"

"I know. But we are here now and seriously, I need you," Kendra had a sad look on her face.

"I'm sorry. I'm here for you, I promise. Now start from the top and don't leave anything out, Kendra!"

"So, remember earlier in the year I went to Virginia for my cousin's funeral?"

"Yeah."

"Well, while I was there, I met a guy."

"And?"

"And we became very interested in one another and kept in contact. At first, it was just phone conversations and then porn-related phone discussions and then when you and "Lover Boy" decided you'd spend a freaking month in paradise; he flew down for a long weekend and let's just say … we never left the house. Hell, we barely left the bed!" Kendra was embarrassed as she told the story to Sherita.

"Hey, don't be blaming your schoolgirl activities on me and Kroy!" Sherita said with a chuckle.

"Hmph, I wish I could say it was just schoolgirl activity and I was able to move on from it," she winced.

"Well, now you're pregnant. Does he know?"

"Yeah. He knows. But it gets worse."

"Worse? What the hell could be worse than getting knocked up by a dude you met at a funeral? Besides, honey, you are well over the legal age to officially screw who you want. And, not to mention, you make a shitload of money that will afford you a pretty decent life as a single mom.

Oh, and let's not forget you have a best friend who will be a "fabulous" godmother. So, tell me exactly how does it get worse? I mean, do you love this guy or something?" Sherita was confused.

As Sherita was talking, Kendra was pulling up the story on her cellphone with Rico's picture. She passed it to her to read.

"What's this?"

"That is him."

"Him, who?"

"The father of my unborn child."

"SHUT THE FRONT DOOR!" Sherita yelled out loud before she knew it, and immediately caught herself once she remembered she was in a public place.

"Wait a minute, Kendra are you telling me that the dude you met at a funeral in Virginia is the same dude whose WIFE is in jail for attempting to kill his ass because she found out he was cheating on her?" Sherita couldn't get the questions out quick enough.

"Yes."

"Kendra! Did you have any idea that he was married?"

"No. I didn't, and I guess I just didn't ask the right types of questions either because I promise you it never came up."

"Well, how often did you speak with him?"

"At first, two or three times a day."

"And not once did he happen to mention that he was MARRIED?"

"NO! Hell, we had discussions about weekend getaways to Miami. I didn't feel like he was hiding anything."

"Well, now we know. His ass was hiding a wife!"

"Sher!"

"Sorry."

"Would you ladies like to order something to eat?" The waitress returned.

"Do you all serve dark liquor this early in the day?" Sherita asked with a serious look on her face.

"Dark liquor?" The waitress was perplexed.

"Ma'am, never mind her, she is delirious. I'll have 1 waffle, 3 strips of turkey bacon, 2 eggs over easy and a small bowl of oatmeal with butter and cinnamon; oh, and a large glass of orange juice and an ice-water."

"Damn, girl, you eating for two or three?" Sherita said in amazement at Kendra's robust food order.

"Shut up, Sher! Now that you know, I can eat what I want."

"Ma'am, would you like anything?" The waitress insisted.

"Just bring me a bowl of fruit and a waffle please. Thank you."

"Seriously? A bowl of fruit?"

"What? I don't intend on gaining sympathy weight with your pregnant ass."

"Whatever."

"So, what did cheater-dude have to say about this baby on the way?"

"Really? You are calling him cheater-dude?"

"Well, what the hell else am I supposed to call him, Kendra? If it will make you feel better, I will refer to him by his government given name."

"Rico. His name is Rico."

"RICO? Is he 12?"

"Huh? What are you talking about?"

"What grown-ass man is named Rico? I already don't like his ass."

"What grown-ass man is named Kroy? Oh, my bad, only an island-accented brother to whom you picked up in a hotel lobby and married him a year later!"

"Touche'; but…"

"But what?"

"I'm NOT pregnant and he WASN'T married."

"Ok, look Sher! I'm sorry, I am not perfect like you, and my life just can't seem to resemble the essence of a romance novel, but I need some support here. I feel like you're mad at me and I just don't need that right now."

"You're right. I'm sorry. What's the plan? Seems like it is raining babies all over my life right now so let me know how "I" can help "YOU" through this?"

"I guess I am going to keep this baby. It looks like I will just have to be a single parent."

"You will not be a single parent. I will be here with you every step of the way. I promise."

"Thanks, Sher."

"Hey, that's what I'm here for."

"So, what'd you mean by its raining babies in your life? Any more news on the baby with Tracy and Josh?"

"Girl, no! That is over and done with, thank God. I think Josh is in a state of anger that won't even let him utter the words date right now. No, but get this, the other day, I received a beautiful bouquet of pink and white roses congratulating me on my first grandchild and surprisingly enough revealing that Alana is pregnant."

"WHAT? OMG Sherita! Are you serious? Is it true?" Kendra blurted out her words while she smeared butter over her waffle.

"Yeah. It appears as if it is, she burst into tears and rattled off some crazy cuckoo explanation that nobody understood. I just don't know what to do about it either. I mean, she's a grown woman and can certainly make her own decisions."

"Wow. Who's the father? Is it a boy from school?"

"I don't know. We didn't get that far yet. She ended up calling Tyrone, wanting to be the one to tell him first."

"Oh my God, how did that go? Is he in ICU after that news?"

"Girl, he blew a gasket and vowed never to speak to her again. She is completely frantic over it. You know how she feels about her dad."

"Yeah, I know. He must be devastated. Have you spoken with him?"

"No. He won't answer his cellphone and that wicked wife of his won't let me speak with him whenever I call the house."

"Well, we all know that bitch is crazy anyway," Kendra said through a mouthful of food.

"I know, right."

The two ate in silence for the next few minutes, both trying desperately to take in the other's news of the day.

"Is everything OK, ladies?" The waitress asked.

Silence.

"Can I get you anything else?" She insisted.

Silence.

"Will this be one check or two?" The waitress asked with a concerned tone.

"One. Thank you," Sherita answered quickly.

"Sher, girl, I got it. I had the news to share."

"Chile, never mind that! I am going to be an Auntie and, therefore, I need to get use to feeding this soon-to-be brat!" she laughed.

"Ha! I guess you're right. But seeing as how you will also be a grandmother at the same time, we will have to come up with a sexy name to call you. Ooh, how 'bout, 'Auntie-Grand'?"

"Go to hell!" Sherita laughed.

After finishing their meals and paying the check, the two ladies stood and hugged as tightly as either of them could stand. They knew they had endured far worse in their history together and this certainly wouldn't get the best of them.

"I love you, Sherita Coleman LaBeauf." "Hmph, not as much as I love you! This is going to be good."

CHAPTER 18

Kendra rushed in the door to her house trying desperately to get to the bathroom.

This whole pregnancy thing was going to take some getting used to. Breathing a sigh of relief, she felt good about finally being able to share her news about the baby with Sherita. She knew that as long as Sherita had her back, she really didn't care what anyone else would have to say about it. She knew deep down her mother would have a few sarcastic remarks. Kendra never could please that woman.

After washing her hands and leaving the bathroom, Kendra clicked on the television. The phone rang.

"Hello."

"You have a collect call from the Nassau County Police Department in New York City, do you accept the charges?" the operator asked on the other end.

"Yes, I accept."

Kendra's heart was beating fast. This was the third collect call she'd received from a county jail in New York. She needed to get to the bottom of this.

"Go ahead with your call ma'am," instructed the operator.

"Hello?" said the nervous voice on the other end of the phone.

"Yes? Who is this?" Kendra asked with caution.

"Perhaps I should be the one asking the questions," the woman responded.

"Wait a minute. If I'm correct, yo' ass just called me collect from what sounds like jail and you got an attitude? Who the fuck is this?" Kendra was quickly becoming indignant.

"Look little missy, I'm the wife of the professor you've been screwing for over a year! And as a result of your disrespectful actions, I'm having to call you from this hellhole. So, you listen up and hear me clearly. I don't know how your Momma raised you, but where I come from you mess with another woman's man you get your ass handed to you on a platter. Perhaps you didn't think I would ever find out about all the late-night study sessions or overnight hotel romps, but the secret is out. You better watch your back, because I've got people watching you," Sabrina's threats were real.

Kendra was stunned. She wasn't sure what she was hearing or if this woman realized she'd contacted the wrong person.

"Well, while I appreciate your scary prison threat, I hate to inform you that I am not in school and I don't live in New York," Kendra said directly.

"Excuse me? Is this not Alana Coleman?"

Speechless, Kendra stopped breathing for a second.

"How do you know, Alana?" she asked calmly.

"The question is how do you know Alana?" Sabrina responded.

"She's, my goddaughter. And I don't think I understand why you're calling my phone, threatening her?"

Sabrina burst out into uncontrollable laughter. She was infuriated to the point that she couldn't even cry. That damn Rico wasn't just cheating on her with one of his students; his dumb ass was cheating on the student with her own godmother.

"Wait a minute. Let me get this correct. So, do you know Rico Harris?"

"Yes."

"But you didn't know that he was having an affair with Alana Coleman?"

"No."

"So, if I am able to put two and two together, it appears as though the plot to this story just got better. You see Miss..."

"Kendra."

"Hmm…. Kendra. I don't know exactly what the connection is to you and Rico, but I can only assume that you are one of the many women he's been spending time with, and as a result, he has somehow managed to involve himself with two women who happen to know each other. Am I correct?"

"Look, I don't know what kind of games you're playing and why you feel like making idle threats is going to make a difference in whatever the hell is going on with you and your out-of-control husband, but I believe this conversation is over," Kendra needed to talk to Alana and quick!

"Wait! Don't hang up."

"You mentioned that you don't live in New York? So, exactly what is your relationship with my husband?" Sabrina asked with sincerity.

"Hmph, he's my baby's daddy," Kendra said with conviction as she hung up the phone.

Heart racing and completely taken aback by the entire conversation, she wasn't sure what to think. Could it be true that Alana had been romantically involved with a married man? Was that man, in fact, Rico? Could he be the unknown father of her child? Kendra was pacing the floor, trying to make sense of it all and the phone rang, it was Alana.

"Hello!"

"Hey Aunt Kendra, is everything alright? You sound out of breath," Alana said as she started the conversation.

"Alana, listen to me. You need to tell me everything that is going on with you and you need to tell me now," Kendra tried to be as calm as possible.

"What do you mean…" Alana tried to speak.

"LISTEN, DON'T GIVE ME NO BULLSHIT! What the hell is going on up in New York, Alana?" Kendra was screaming.

Alana was scared and tears started streaming down her face.

"Aunt Kendra, I'm pregnant by my married professor," she burst out with uncontrollable sobs on the other end of the phone.

Kendra sat down slowly on the side of the bed as she listened to Alana's tearful story of her year-long relationship with Rico.

Kendra was emotionally torn by the entire situation because she instantly realized that as fate would have it, she and her 21-year-old goddaughter were pregnant by the same man. Taking a deep breath, she felt like she was in a bad episode of a Twilight movie.

"Ok, Alana honey, calm down. Does Rico know you're pregnant?"

"Yes. He knows and he offered me money for an abortion."

"ABORTION!"

"Yeah, abortion. He said that a baby wasn't in his plans for his life and that he needed to focus his attention on his wife."

"That motherfucker got a lot of goddamn nerve suggesting you have an abortion! Is he crazy? I wish the hell he would've suggested some shit like that to me," Kendra was heated.

"Don't worry, I told him to keep his money. I don't need him to help me with anything. I am sure I will figure this out on my own."

"Sweetie, you don't have to figure anything out on your own. Your Mom and I will be here with you every step of the way, no matter what your decision is. But you are going to have to tell your mom and your dad the truth about who the father is sooner rather than later."

"I know. My dad hates me. I ruined my life and he's never going to speak to me again," Alana cried.

"No, no honey. He doesn't hate you. He's just a bit disappointed right now, but he could never hate you. You're his baby-girl and he is just in shock. Give him some time, he'll come around."

"I don't know, I've managed to screw this up royally and I may not be able to bounce back. What should I do?"

"Hmph. Hold on."

"Wait, what are you doing?"

"Calling your mother."

"My mother? Why? Aunt Kendra!"

Kendra clicked over and took a deep breath as she called Sherita's cellphone. This whole thing has become twisted quickly and everything needed to be out in the open so that there wasn't any confusion. This family was about to be rocked to the core and Kendra wasn't going to let this destroy their lives.

187

"Alana, you there?" Kendra asked as she clicked back over.

"Yeah. I'm here, but I don't…." she was interrupted when Josh answered Sherita's cellphone.

"Chelloooo," Josh answered in a playful singing tone.
"Josh, honey, it's Aunt Kendra. Is your mom around?"

"What's up, Aunt Kendra? How you doin' today?"

"I've seen better days, but OK for the most part. Where's your mom?"

"Oh, she right here in the kitchen. Hold on a minute. Mom, Aunt Kendra's on the phone and she's acting really weird," Josh forewarned his mother.

"Boy, give me the phone!"

"Hey girl, what's up?"

"Sher, I need to talk to you."

"OK. Is everything alright? I mean, when we spoke earlier, and you had this tone, you ended up telling me you were pregnant. Should I sit down for this news?"

"Yes. You should definitely sit."

"Alright," Sherita did as she was instructed and sat down at the kitchen table with Josh staring at her from across the room with an inquisitive look.

"Mom, did you just say Aunt Kendra was PREGNANT?" he whispered with a look of shock and confusion on his face.

Sherita quickly lifted her finger to her mouth telling him to be quiet.

"Alright, spill it Kendra, what's going on?"

"First, let me say that I have Alana on the phone as well."

"Alana? Why? What's she doing on the phone?"

"Hey mommy," Alana was shaking she was so nervous, she wasn't sure what Kendra's plan was for this call.

"Hey honey, are you OK?"

"Yeah, Ma, I'm fine."

"Kendra, out with it!"

"Wait, Lan is on the phone, too? Ma, what are they doing?" Josh was becoming anxious in the background.

Sherita gave him a stern look, which he understood to mean he needed to sit down and shut-up while she tried to figure it out. She waved her arm in a "go-away" motion at Josh as she listened intently. At that moment, Kroy walked into the kitchen.

"Oh Lord, what's going on in here?" Kroy asked once he recognized the "shit's-bout-to-happen" look from both Josh and Sherita.

"Sher, so let me figure out where to begin?"

"From the top is where it will make the most sense," Sherita interjected.

"OK, so you know how earlier today we were at breakfast, and I shared with you my GLORIOUS news about being pregnant, and the not-so-glorious part about it being from a man who I barely knew; and I met him at a funeral in Virginia nearly a year ago?" Kendra was rambling.

"Yeah?"

"Well, after we left the spot this morning I came home, and I had to pee like a mutha…."

"Get to the point, Kendra!"

"Yeah, right. So, I got another collect call today from an inmate at the Nassau County Police Department in New York. You remember, I told you I had been getting these random collect calls but didn't accept any of them because I don't know nobody in New York, let alone in a county jail. But anyway, that's neither here nor there. So, today, I accepted the call, because I needed to figure out why this person kept calling me and to inform them that they seemingly had the wrong number."

"OK?"

Alana gasped as Kendra continued her story.

"Well, the inmate on the other end of the phone just so happened to be the wife of the guy that I was telling you about earlier."

"KENDRA! SHUT THE FRONT DOOR! What did she say?" Sherita all of a sudden forgot Alana was even on the phone.

"Well, see, that's where it gets interesting."

"What do you mean? Interesting?"

"She really wasn't looking for me."

"So, how'd she get your number?"

"She thought I was Alana."

"WHAT? She thought you were Alana? Why would she call you looking for Alana and better yet, WHY would she even know Alana?"

"Alana?" Kendra said calmly.

"Mommy, I've been having an affair with my married professor."

Stunned beyond belief, Sherita dropped the phone on the floor as she nearly fell out of her seat.

Luckily, Kroy broke her fall and caught her before she hit the ground.

"MA!" Josh yelled.

"OH MY GOD, Mi' AMORE!!" Kroy cried out as he caught his wife before she injured herself.

"What is going on!?" Josh asked as he picked up the phone from the floor.

Hearing loud sobs and crying in the background, Josh tried to make sense of it all.

"Aunt Kendra! Hello! Lan? Are you guys, OK? What is going on? Will somebody please talk to me?" Josh was frantic.

Kroy managed to stabilize Sherita back in the chair. Watching her facial expressions intently, he needed to make sure she was OK.

"I'm fine. I'm fine. Where is the phone?" Sherita said insistently as she snapped back into reality.

"Josh, give me the damn phone!" she yelled.

"Why the hell is everybody crying? What did they say to you, Ma?" Josh asked as he handed back the phone.

"Kendra, Alana you both need to calm down, right this minute. I need some clarity! Let me see if I understand correctly. Alana, you've been sleeping with your married professor who just so happens to be the man plastered all over the news for his wife attempting to KILL him for cheating? And as fate would have it, he is the same SCUM BAG that you, Kendra, met at a funeral nearly a year ago.

And it turns out that both of you are PREGNANT from this SAME ASSHOLE whose wife is in county lock up calling random phone numbers looking for my daughter because she has some vendetta to settle!" Sherita was yelling at the top of her lungs.

Stunned and unable to move, Josh and Kroy both looked at each other in amazement as they tried to follow the story in their heads.

"Yeah, that's pretty much it in a nutshell," Kendra said sarcastically.

"Mom, I'm sorry!" Alana sobbed in the phone.

"Shut the hell up, Kendra! Alana you should be sorry!"

"Boy, your dad is going to be none-too-happy about this," Kroy said softly in his heavy-island accent as he headed out of the kitchen and soothingly tapped Josh's shoulder.

"I need a drink and I am going to have to talk to you two ladies later. Don't call me. I'll call you," Sherita said calmly as she hung up the phone.

"Mom…."

Sherita raised her hand motioning for silence.

"Not now Josh. Not now."

Chapter 19

Sabrina stared at the headset of the payphone in amazement. Did she say, "her baby-daddy"?

Was this woman pregnant by her husband? The swirl of thoughts going through her head was making her nauseous. She needed to speak with Kendra again and this time, ask some in-depth questions about her relationship with Rico. This 404-area code was the only phone number she ever remembered seeing in Rico's phone, and she made it a point to memorize it because she knew one day, she would need to confront the bitch who was sleeping with her husband.

She assumed it was Alana's phone number since she was the only person, she knew of that Rico had been spending countless hours with day and night. She needed some answers and she needed them now.

"Guard!"

"Yeah. What's up? Are you done with your call?"

"Um, for some reason we got disconnected and the operator suggested that I re-dial the call. Is it OK if I have 5 more minutes to try back?"

"You've got 5 minutes and then you're going back to your cell."

"Thank you. I promise, I will be quick."

"Hurry up!"

With no time to spare, Sabrina quickly dialed Rico's number. Waiting on him to pick up, she knew her time would be limited once the operator finished her spiel.

"Hello."

"You have a collect call from an inmate at the Nassau County Police Department, do you accept the charge," the operator sounded like a recorded message.

"Um, yeah. Yes, I accept," Rico said stuttering as he sat up in the chair.

"Sabrina! Baby, are you OK?"

"Don't baby me, asshole. I don't have but a minute to talk. You need to come see me tomorrow between 1 to 3 p.m. for visitation."

"Ok. I'll be there. Is there anything you need?"
"Yeah. The truth," she said as she hung up the phone.

Sabrina headed down the hall to wait for the guard to escort her back to her cell. She needed the truth, and it had to come from Rico.

CHAPTER 20

Bella was anxious and sad all at the same time during the cab ride to the airport. The time had finally come for Hustle to return to California. She had caused more than her fair share of drama in the month that she'd been in New York. Bella felt like she needed to get her life back and release from Hustle's jealous tendencies. The last couple of days had been strenuous and the two really hadn't talked much.

"I guess you're still mad at me?" Hustle asked.

"I'm just ready for all of this to be over."

"Bella, I never meant to hurt you so much."

"Yeah, well, I never thought you would either. But I guess I was wrong."

"Now that's not fair. I love you, Bella. I have always loved you and I don't ever want to do anything that causes you pain."

"Well, you sure have a strange way of showing it. WHY Hustle? Why did you feel like you needed to send Alana's mom flowers? Was it any business of yours to get involved? HUH?"

The cab driver peered at the two women through his rearview mirror. They were only five minutes away from the airport and hopefully these two wouldn't break out into a fist fight before they arrived.

"Look, Bella, it is no secret that Alana and I don't get along with one another."

"That is no reason for you to go getting involved with something that has absolutely nothing to do with you, Hustle."

"You're right. I should've just stayed out of it. But I felt like she was taking you away from me and she needed to be put back in her place."

"Taking me away from you? Are you crazy? You don't own me, Hustle! Alana is my friend. She is the only person I've met who cares about me for me. She doesn't care that I am gay or that my hair is multicolored or that I smoke cigarettes, she just cares about me. I've never had that in my life from nobody. Not even you."

"Are you saying I don't care about you, Bella?"

"I'm saying you care more about yourself than you do me at times. I am tired of it and I am not going to continue feeling this way about this relationship."

"So, what are you saying?"

The driver pulled up in front of the Atlantic Airlines curbside baggage area.

"That will be $45.50."

Bella handed the driver a 50-dollar bill.

"Keep the change."

"'Preciate it. Do you need a ride back to the city?"

"No, thank you."

The two headed inside to the kiosks for check-in. Hustle handled her business at the counter and checked the two bags she'd brought with her. Bella waited patiently.

"All set."

"Good."

"Look, Bella…"

"Hustle, it's OK. We've known for quite some time that this day would come. I just hate that we had to have such division between us when it did. I love you and I will always have a huge place in my heart for you, but I just feel it's best that we go our separate ways."

"So, this is it, huh? You just gonna end it here in the airport? You couldn't have told me this before we left the apartment or yesterday or two days ago?"

"I'm sorry."

"Yeah. Me, too."

Hustle was hurt and angry. She brushed strongly up against Bella's arm as she passed her.
With tears in her eyes, she headed toward security. Bella sat down on the nearest bench and cried. She loved Hustle but knew that this relationship was too toxic.

She should've ended it 2 years ago before she left for New York. Her life was different now and with the growth and maturity she'd experienced in the past year, she needed to move on.

Bella looked at her cellphone, it was 2:30 p.m. she got up and headed toward the subway station. It would be a long ride home, but it would be well worth it. She needed to clear her head.

CHAPTER 21

Sherita sat silently in the chair beside her bed gazing out the window at the beautiful sunrise.
She hadn't slept a wink.

All she could think about was Alana and how scared she must be. However, she was also furious with her daughter and felt that all of this was somehow her fault. Didn't she teach her better than to get involved with a married man?

As her thoughts swirled around in her head, she grew angry at the notion of Rico manipulating her baby into his web of lies and deceit. She'd tried to call Tyrone a few times during the past couple of days, but he didn't respond. She really needed to talk to him. She understood that he was hurt and upset, but they needed to pull it together and figure this out. In that instance, Sherita became overwhelmed with grief. She decided she was going to put this family back on track and fast. She looked over at Kroy, who was asleep in bed. She got up and tiptoed lightly into the bathroom. She dressed quietly and hurriedly, not to wake him.

As she grabbed her purse off the dresser, she glanced quickly at the clock beside the bed on the nightstand. It was 6:20 a.m. and the only way to get Tyrone to talk to her was going to be face-to-face.

Sherita hopped in her car and headed toward Tyrone and Felicia's house. Their daughter was in trouble and she needed them together in unity to help get her through this.

As she headed down the highway, she reflected back on times when things seemed simple. Alana and Josh had grown up so fast, and she just wanted to keep them protected for as long as she could.

206

As she pulled up to the house, she prepared her mind for what the confrontation would be like.

Knock, knock, knock….

The house was dark, and the morning breeze was chilly standing on the porch. She tried again.

Knock, knock, knock….

"Who is it?" Tyrone yelled through the door.

"Ty, it's me, Sherita."

"Sherita?"

Unlocking the door, Tyrone opened up with a look of confusion on his face.

"Woman do you know what time it is? What 'da hell are you doing out this early in the morning knocking on folks' doors? You almost got shot!"

"Well, if you'd return my phone calls, I wouldn't have to be out this early in the morning disturbing the peace," she shot back.

"Get in here. What is this about, Sher?"

"It's about your daughter. She…"

"She what, Sher? She doesn't need a damn thing from me. She made that decision when she decided to go and get knocked up her last year in college," Tyrone said with pain in his face.

"Ty, look, I get it. She fucked up and she knows it, but how long are you going to play this 'Daddy don't care' role?

"For as long as I need to. Hell, until I get over this shit."

"Well, hopefully you'll give yourself a sooner-rather-than-later timeframe because she's in deeper than we thought, and right now she needs our help, Ty."

"What are you talking about, Sher?"

"Promise me you won't fly off the handle."

"I ain't promising shit. Now what the hell is going on?"

Just as Sherita was about to share her news with Tyrone, Felicia appeared at the top of the steps with her arms crossed and a look of fire in her eyes.

"This bitch," Sherita said to herself as she rolled her eyes at the thought of the exchange that was about to take place.
"What are you doing in my house?" Felicia asked dryly.

"Good morning, Felicia! Hey, listen, my sincerest apologies for stopping by so early in the morning but, Tyrone here hadn't returned any of my phone calls and I figured this would be the best way for me to have a quick chat with him.

You don't mind do you, hun?" Sherita's sarcastically chipper disposition was only fueling the fire.

"Felicia, honey, go back to bed. Sherita won't be here long," Tyrone insisted.

"Yeah, honey, go back to bed. I won't be here long," Sherita said with a forced smile.

"Ty, when is this shit going to end? She calls every damn day and now she's showing up at my house! What the fuck is going on with you two?" she asked.

"Look Tyrone, I just need 5 minutes to talk to you about Alana and I am out of your hair. I didn't come here to cause trouble and I certainly don't feel like getting into a shouting match with your paranoid princess."

"Felicia, I got it. Make it quick, Sher."

Tyrone stepped to the side and gestured toward the living room offering Sherita a seat. She sat down and got right to the point.

"OK, so, it seems as though Alana has gotten caught up with one of her professors at school."

"What?"

"Yeah. And if that isn't enough, he's married, and I believe he is the father of her baby."

"MARRIED? ARE YOU FUCKING KIDDING ME?" Tyrone raised his voice.

"I wish I were. But I'm not. It gets worse."

"Worse?" Tyrone asked with his eyes closed as he massaged his temples.

"Not sure if you've watched the news lately regarding the wife in New York who is currently facing charges for allegedly trying to kill her husband after she found out he'd been cheating on her?"

"Yeah…"

"Well, he's the cheating husband and she's the shooter wife."

"How'd this happen, Sherita?"

"That's not all…"

"There's more?"

"As fate would have it, he's the same dude that Kendra met nearly a year ago at a cousin's funeral in Virginia. They've been having a long-distance relationship off and on for a few months, and, as a result, Kendra is 10-weeks pregnant as well."

"BY THE SAME GUY?"

"Yeah. Same guy."

"This shit is unbelievable! How do you know it's the same guy?"

"You ready for this?"

"No."

"The wife has been calling Kendra collect from jail for the past two weeks and she never answered until yesterday.

Once they started talking, the wife thought she was calling to confront Alana, when, in fact, it was Kendra's phone and just so happen they both are connected to one another."

"Unbeknownst to the wife," he chimed in.

"Yep. She had no idea. Apparently, she's been going through his phone and memorized the most constant unfamiliar number, which so happened to be Kendra's, but apparently she knew or had some knowledge of Alana and his interaction with her and just assumed that it was her number."

"You guys should write a book about this madness," Tyrone joked.

"Tell me about it. I could write a book about my entire twisted life," she snickered.

"So, what do we need to do, Sherita?"

"We need to talk to Alana. Face-to-face…"

"OK. I'll book us a flight for tomorrow," he said with a deep breath.

"Thanks Ty."

The two stood and shared an awkward hug. Tyrone desperately needed to fight these familiar feelings he had for Sherita. He loved Felicia and he had to leave the past in the past. Witnessing the embrace, Felicia made her presence known by loudly clearing her throat.

"Your 5 minutes are up. I want you out of my house," she said.

Throwing her hands up in surrender, Sherita complied and headed for the door with a sarcastic smile on her face.

CHAPTER 22

Kroy was sitting at the kitchen table drinking a cup of coffee and reading the newspaper.

"Hey. What's up Kroy?" Josh said as he entered the room.

"Hey Josh. Morning."

"Any idea where my mom went?"

"No. I was about to ask you the same thing. She was gone when I got up this morning."

"There is some weird stuff happening' round here."

"Hmph, I know what you mean."

"Hey, do you mind giving me a ride to work?"

"Yeah, sure. What's going on with your truck?"

"Honestly, I haven't had a minute to even think about the truck since the accident. It is still running hot and that is driving me bananas. I really need to talk to my dad about getting me a new car."

"Have you taken it to a mechanic?"

"No. I don't have the money for that right now. And since I haven't worked in a couple weeks, I am really living off of nickels and dimes until I get some hours under my belt."

"I hear you. Well, maybe when you get off work today or tomorrow, we can bring it to a mechanic and get it checked out. I'll cover the cost."

"Really? Yo, thanks man. I appreciate that. I will pay you back."

"No worries. I don't need you to pay me back."

"Thanks man. Hey, let me grab a bowl of cereal and then I will be ready to roll. Is that OK?"

"Yeah, just let me know."

Kroy headed to the bedroom to shower and get dressed. He and Josh were slowly building a relationship with each other. He respected his stepchildren and wanted to show them that he cared about them and that they could depend on him in their life. One of the things he loved the most about Sherita was her commitment to her kids and her family. She reminded him a lot of his mother. In that instance, he realized it had been a while since he spoke to his own mother and decided to call home once he got dressed.

"Bonjour Momma, comment allez-vous?"

"Oh! Bonjour mon fils! Comment allez-vous? Long time no parler, on commencait a se' preoccuper de vous."

"Oh, no worries, Momma. I am fine. How is Poppa doing?" Kroy smiled as he spoke with his mother.

"Your father is fine, son. He is working too hard, but that is what he loves to do."

"Yes. I know."

"We miss you son. Is everything OK for you?"

"Yes, we are well here. Sherita has been a bit pre-occupied with the kids, but otherwise we are good."

"Oh, how is my beautiful daughter-in-law? How are the kids? When are you guys going to bring them to Trinidad for us to spend time with them?"

"Momma, we will soon. I promise. You know, Alana is off at school in New York and Josh, he works, so we will have to work on coordinating a time when we can all come and stay a couple of weeks."

"That would be wonderful. You know we miss you tremendously here on the island."

"I know. I miss you guys, too."

Knock knock…

"Hey Kroy, you ready?" Josh asked as he stuck his head in the door.

"Yeah. Be right out," Kroy replied as he looked up at Josh standing in the door.

"Momma, I've got to go and take Josh to work now. Give everyone my love and hugs and tell them I will see them soon, OK. Tell Poppa, I will call him soon to speak with him as well."

"OK, son. Je t'aime de tout mon Coeur."

"Hmph, I love you, too, Mom," Kroy said with a smile.

Hanging up, Kroy realized he missed his family. It was tough being so far away from them, but he loved his wife and desperately wanted to make it work. Understandably, the past few weeks Sherita had been all wrapped up in the activities of the kids and her ex, but at some point, she was going to have to let them live their own lives. Kroy was being patient, but he was growing weary.

"Ready to go?" Kroy asked Josh.

"Yep."

"By the way, my mom sends her love."

"Cool. Is that who you were speaking French with on the phone?"

"Yes. She speaks limited English."

"I think that is awesome. I would love to learn how to speak French."

"I could teach you."

"Really?"

"Yes, really. It isn't that difficult. It is more repetitive than anything."
"That would be great!"

"OK then. We can start next week."

"Perfect. That way when I go to Trinidad I can speak to the ladies on the beach fluently," Josh chuckled at the thought.

"That's exactly right. They will be impressed."

"Hey, can I go with you to Trinidad the next time you visit?"

"Sure, you can. My familia would love that! They have been begging for you and your sister to come and visit for quite some time now. You'd enjoy it."

"What's it like?"

"Paradise."

"When do we leave?" Josh asked slyly with a grin.

Kroy laughed out loud at Josh's enthusiasm about visiting Trinidad. It made him feel good that he wanted to visit his family and get involved with his culture. Maybe it was time for him to teach Josh how to speak French. He could then teach him about the family business of high-quality art brokering. Then, who knows, this might be something he takes an interest in and could become quite successful doing. He could then travel to Trinidad and all the South American countries running the family business.

Chapter 23

"Wee wee, my friends. Did you miss me?" Josh boasted as he entered the Foot Locker store at Greenbriar Mall.

"Wee Wee? Man, it's worse than we thought! You ain't even speaking English no more after that accident, huh?" joked his co-worker, Corey.

"What up, man? How you been?" Josh was glad to see his friend.

"Man, working like a Hebrew slave covering your shifts. For real, how you feeling?"

"I'm blessed. Just happy to be alive. Y'all been busy?"

"Busy is an understatement," Corey said. "We've been running sales like crazy, and folks have been in here nonstop."

"Word? That's what's up. Well, I am glad to be back, bruh."

"Yeah man, glad to have you back."

"JOSH!"

"Uh-oh, I guess Ms. Sheryl knows I'm back."

"Yep," Corey said with a smile.

"Yes Ma'am? How you doing, Ms. Sheryl?" Josh turned to greet his boss.

"Honey, I'm fine. You alright? I am so sorry to hear that you were in an accident. Did you get the balloons and stuff we sent to the hospital?"

"Yes, ma'am I did. Thank you so much, I really appreciated it. Guess you kind of missed me, huh?" Josh said with a grin.

"Missed you? Boy, get a life! You had us 'round here one man down is what we missed," Ms. Sheryl said sarcastically.

"OK, I hear you."

"So, where you want me at today?"

"I need you covering zones 1 and 2. We still have a huge sale going on and we will be busy, so be sure to greet every customer and push all sale items, especially the BOGO T-shirts in the back."

"Gotcha."

"Alright, let me know if you need to take a break or anything. I don't want to have to perform CPR or something on you today," she joked.

"I'm good, Ms. Sheryl. But I'll let you know," Josh laughed. He was glad to be back at work. He missed his friends.

Chapter 24

Tyrone and Felicia sat in silence at the breakfast table. He knew she was still pissed behind Sherita's unexpected visit. How was he going to share the news that the two of them would be traveling to New York for a few days to check on Alana? He was upset at all that was going on, but what could he do? They were still his children and he wanted to help steer them in the right direction as best he could.

Tyrone was hurt by Alana getting pregnant and by a married man. He knew that a baby wasn't necessarily the end of the world, it just wasn't the vision he had for his daughter this early in life.

"Honey," he said as he cleared his throat.

Felicia remained silent. She cut her eyes at Tyrone from across the table ready to attack at any moment.

"Honey, first let me apologize to you for Sherita just showing up here at the house this morning. I should've called her back and all of this could have been avoided," he said.

"Ty, I really don't think I want to hear your sorry-ass apology. I am so sick and tired of the back and forth with you and that woman to the point where I am just about fed up."

"Sweetie, I know, and I promise it will not be like this much longer."

"Much longer? Are you on drugs, Tyrone? The two of you are so freaking consumed in your grown-ass children's lives that you don't even realize it is the one thing that keeps the two of you joined at the hip, making it damn near impossible for you to move on with your own lives."

"Felicia, that's not true. Sherita and I have worked hard over the years to show our kids love and support; and just because they are young adults doesn't mean that we should just stop caring about their well-being and the decisions they make in life."

"Don't get me wrong Tyrone, I love your children. I think they are smart and intelligent and very well-mannered despite their mother's actions. My issue is with her. The two of you seem to not completely be ready to let go of this relationship you've conjured up over the years interacting with one another, and that is a huge problem. Now, I suggest you guys sit down face-to-face and you explain to her that you no longer want to have contact with her. Your children are old enough that you can interact directly with them; she doesn't need to be involved ever again."

"Felicia, you are being unreasonable. Now I understand that Sherita can be a bit of a diva, and, at times, she forces her ways on the situation without taking into consideration all parties involved, but I don't know that we will ever be able to stop communicating."

"Why not?"

"Because that is just not how our relationship works. Honey, listen, I love you. I've made some terrible mistakes here lately and I truly apologize for that, but no doubt about it, you are the only one in my life that matters. Sherita is the mother of my children, and I can't change that, but that is all she means to me."

"Ty, the other night you called out her name just as we were about to make love. You really expect me to think that there isn't something more to this scenario? Do you take me for some sort of fool?"

Tyrone was busted. He and Felicia hadn't talked about that incident since it happened. He really wasn't trying to call out Sherita's name that day, it just sort of happened. This was something that had him equally as perplexed as it did Felicia.

"I can only apologize for that day. You are right. I have no excuse for my actions. I cannot sit here and tell you that I don't love my ex-wife because I do. She has been in my life for nearly 30 years and it's just not something you sweep under a

rug easily. But what I can say to you, and I give you my word, give us a few weeks to help Alana get on track with this drama in her life and I promise you I will have that talk with Sherita and if you still want me to cut all ties with her, then I guess I will have no other choice. Felicia, I love you and I am in love with you and the last thing I want is for us to be at odds over something that can be fixed."

"I only want to see her face in pictures," Felicia meant business.

"I hear you. Now, I do have to share with you that the reason she came here this morning was because it appears as though Alana is in more trouble than just being pregnant, she could possibly be in danger. Sherita and I have decided we need to go to New York and get to the bottom of everything that is taking place."

"And?" she asked with her arms crossed as she leaned back in her chair.

"And she and I are going to fly to New York first thing tomorrow and stay a couple of days to get things on track for Alana?"

"WHAT? Do you think I am going to agree to you going out of town with that witch and stay a couple of days? Absolutely not, I will not allow it!"

"Wait a minute, what do you mean you will not allow it? First of all, I am a grown-ass man, and I don't respond favorably to anybody telling me what they will and won't allow me to do for my kids. Now I understand your frustration and I get the fact that Sherita is not at the top of your friends and family list, but sweetheart, this you are going to have to trust me on," Tyrone stated firmly.

"Fine Tyrone, go ahead to New York. Do whatever your heart desires."

Felicia stood and put her coffee mug in the sink and headed back upstairs without another word. She was pissed and Tyrone knew that he was taking a huge gamble with his marriage, but what else could he do? It was his baby girl.

Sherita and Kroy pulled up in the driveway at the same time. Perplexed about where he could be coming from, she hopped out the car all smiles.

"Hey honey, good morning," she said as she greeted him with a kiss on the lips.

"Sherita, where've you been?" he asked.

Sherita grabbed Kroy's hand and headed toward the house.

"I couldn't sleep this morning thinking about Alana and I really needed to talk to Tyrone, so I dropped by their house."

"You dropped by Tyrone and Felicia's house this early in the morning because you couldn't sleep?"

"Well, that isn't the reason, honey. I've been trying to speak with Ty by phone for days and I really need him to know what is going on with Alana."

Kroy sat down at the table in the kitchen. He knew that it was time he voiced his uneasiness with Sherita and her relationship with Tyrone.

"Mon Amore' listen, we need to talk. Now, I understand that as a parent you are always concerned for the well-being of your children and you have every right to be, but it is time for you two to let go of Alana and Josh and let them face the music on their own."

"What? What are you talking about? We do let them do stuff on their own," Sherita became defensive.

"No, you don't. Sweetie, I am sorry to tell you this, but you are more often than not way too controlling when it comes to your kids and sometimes you have to be willing to let them figure it out no matter how difficult it seems."

"With all due respect Kroy, the last I checked your kids are back home in paradise, therefore, you don't have the right to talk to me about how to support mine."

Leaning back in the chair and raising his hands up in a surrender pose, Kroy recognized quickly that this conversation was about to head in the wrong direction.

"Look, Sherita, with all due respect to you, I think you are an excellent mother, and your kids are great kids. Unfortunately, they are not perfect and will make some pretty bad mistakes. This situation with Alana is one of them. However, she is an adult who chose to make adult decisions about her interaction with a person of the opposite sex and as a result there is a consequence. You, my love, cannot fix this even if you had a magic wand."

"Well, what do you suggest I do, Kroy? Should I just leave her alone to have this baby all by herself?"

"No, I am not saying that."

"Then what the hell are you saying?" she yelled.

"I am saying, she got herself into this mess, she needs to figure out how to get out of it. You don't have to run off and save the world every time a dark cloud hovers over your children. Not to mention you are putting Tyrone in an awkward position with choosing to be there either for you or for them."

"I do not! Tyrone loves his kids!"

"And he loves you, too, but give the man a chance to move forward with his life and stop involving him in stuff that you yourself shouldn't be caught up in!" Kroy was yelling.

Sherita sat with her head in her hands. Kroy was right. She did get too involved where Josh and Alana were concerned. Maybe she and Tyrone should let Alana figure this out on her own and just be there to help pick up the pieces, if needed. As she sat staring across the table at her husband, the phone rang, it was Tyrone. She answered it on speaker.

"Hey Ty."

"Sher, I don't know if it's a good idea for us to go to New York together. Felicia is paranoid about the whole situation and to be honest, I don't want to cause any more friction between the two of us than there already is. Now, if you want to still go, I am happy to pay for the flight and hotel for a couple of days."

"Hey Tyrone, it's Kroy. That won't be necessary, I can take care of my wife's travel arrangements."

"Hey Kroy, what's up. My bad man, I didn't realize I was on speaker phone."

"No problem."

"I understand and I didn't mean any disrespect."

"Listen, guys, enough," Sherita interjected. "Ty, you're right. I don't want to create any additional tension in your household or mine," she said, peering into Kroy's eyes.

"I will go to New York myself and find out what is going on with Alana and let you know as soon as I know something. I will reach out to you in a couple of days."

Sherita ended the call without saying goodbye. Life needed to move forward, and it needed to happen now.

"Mon Amore, I am going with you. I will make all the arrangements," Kroy kissed his wife on the forehead as he headed toward the bedroom.

He knew this was difficult for her, but he loved her enough to work through the madness with her.

"OK."

Chapter 25

Alana felt miserable. Morning sickness was making it difficult for her to concentrate in class and all throughout the day. She had been somewhat distant for the past two days just trying to wrap her head around all that was happening. How did she get here in life? What was she going to do with a baby? She laid across the bed in a daze staring at the ceiling as she gently rubbed her hand across her stomach. All she could think about was her dad and how angry he was that she was pregnant. Hopefully he still loved her, she thought.

Meanwhile, back home in Atlanta, Kendra looked at the clock and realized she needed to get ready for work. The trouble with being pregnant was that she was starting to show and could barely fit into anything that didn't resemble a bed sheet. She hadn't talked to Sherita in a day or two and truthfully was embarrassed and not sure how the conversation would go. She wanted to speak with Alana but wasn't sure how to share her own innermost feelings surrounding the reality that the two of them were both carrying Rico's baby.

In all her years, she never thought she'd be in this type of situation. As both ladies daydreamed about the reality of their current situation, they both thought of each other. Life sure does have a way of taking you on a rollercoaster ride, Kendra thought to herself as she got dressed for work.

Sherita and Kroy settled into their Manhattan hotel and decided to grab a bite to eat near NYU's campus. Sherita didn't tell Alana she was coming in hopes that she wouldn't give her pause for concern. As they sat waiting for their food to arrive, Sherita noticed a gentleman sitting across the room shuffling through some papers in a manila folder.

"Mon Amore, is everything OK? You look like you've seen a ghost," Kroy asked as he casually gazed around the room attempting to identify what had caught his wife's attention.

"Umm, I'm not quite sure, but I think that guy over there looks familiar."

"Do you know people in New York, honey?"

"Not very many, but I can't help but think I know him."

As their food arrived, Sherita couldn't take her eyes off the seemingly preoccupied gentleman from across the room.

"Excuse me," she asked the waitress. "Do you by chance know that gentleman sitting at that table over there?"

Peering across the room, the waitress quickly identified the person Sherita was asking about.
"Oh, yeah, that is Professor Harris. He teaches African American Studies at NYU. I had him a couple of semesters ago; he's in here just about every day before class. Nice guy. He's got a lot going on right now, but he seems pretty cool. Why? Do you know him?"

Sherita's hands started to sweat as she quickly realized that this was the man who had managed to disrupt the lives of both her daughter and her best friend. And the nerve of him to just be out in public eating in a restaurant as if all is well in his world.

"Hmph, African Studies huh?" she asked inquisitively.

"Yes ma'am."

"Thank you. By the way, what did you mean when you mentioned that he has "a lot" going on right now?"

"Well, unfortunately he's been all over the news lately. Seems like there is a nasty rumor going around on campus that he's been involved with a female student and that his wife found out and that news didn't go over so well."

"Wow. Interesting, and yet he looks so innocent," Sherita was fuming inside.

"Yeah but looks can be deceiving. Well, enjoy your lunch. Let me know if you need anything."

"We will. Thanks."

"Mon Amore, what are you thinking?" Kroy recognized the look on his wife's face.

"Nothing honey, eat your salad. I'll be right back."

"What? Where are you going? Sherita…"

Before Kroy had a chance to react, Sherita had left the table. She walked toward the table where the gentleman was sitting so, she could get a closer look as she hid in the hallway near the restrooms within eyeshot of Rico. She was nervous. What should she do? She decided to call Kendra.

"Hello?"

"Kendra! It's me Sher..." she said whispering.

"Sher? Girl, why are you whispering what's wrong?"

"Look, I don't have much time and I need to talk fast."

"What? Where are you? What are you doing?" Kendra was confused.

"Kendra, I am in a restaurant standing near the restrooms literally about 10 feet away from yo' baby's daddy."

"Huh? Sherita, girl, you are trippin'. What are you talking about? Where are you?"

"Look! I don't have time to explain. Kroy and I flew to New York this morning to see Alana and decided to get lunch before we went to her apartment. Long story short, as fate would have it, we just so happen to be at the VERY restaurant that your cheating ass baby daddy eats at every day and I am literally standing here watching him from across the room," Sherita said quickly.

"WHAT?!"

"Sherita! What are you going to do?"

"I don't know. Unfortunately, this wasn't written into my plan once I arrived in New York, but I feel like I need to do something."

"Ok, Sher, listen to me. I don't think he knows that Alana and I have a connection. So be very careful what you do and what you say."

"Yeah, yeah, yeah…. I got you. OOOHH, LET ME CALL YOU BACK, LOOKS LIKE HE'S TRYING TO LEAVE!" Sherita hung up abruptly.

"SHER! SHER…."

Sherita needed to do something and do it quick. As she approached the table, she could see that Rico was preparing to pay his check as he slid his credit card inside the black receipt holder.

She approached the table.

"Hello sir. Was everything OK with your meal today?" She said with a smile as she picked up the black holder.

Looking up, Rico was caught off guard seeing Sherita standing before him. Realizing that he'd never seen her before, he just assumed she was a new manager.

"Um, everything was good. Thank you."

"Good. Let me take care of this for you. I will be right back," she said with a smile as she rushed off with the card holder in hand. She searched around the restaurant for the waitress who helped her and rushed up to her.

"Hey. Listen – I need you to do me a huge favor. I need to speak with that gentleman at that table for a few minutes in private.

Here is his check, but I want you to give me about 10 minutes before you run it and bring it to the table, OK?"

"Umm, OK," the waitress responded perplexed.

Sherita headed back to Rico's table. Her heart was beating outside of her chest. She had no idea what she would say to this man, but she knew she needed to keep calm. Just as she pulled out the chair across from Rico, Kroy noticed her from across the room and was stunned.

"Oh, dear Lord," he thought to himself.

"Hi again. How are you?" she was nervous as she sat down.

"Excuse me, do I know you?" Rico asked with an instant show of annoyance on his face.

"Well, no, you don't actually know me, but I assure you that after what I am about to say you're going to wish that I didn't know you."

"Look, lady, I don't know who you are or what you're doing but I am going to suggest you get up from my table and head back to where you came from before this becomes more than you can handle."

"Yeah, well you see, here's the thing. I am the mother of the pregnant student you've been sleeping with, and I am VERY ready to handle you in whatever way I need to," Sherita shot back.

Looking around the room to see if he was being punked, Rico was stunned at Sherita's actions.

"What? You are trippin'. You don't know me!"

"You're right, I don't know you, but my daughter sure does. And how do you think things will go for you if your 15 minutes of fame continues in the media when news gets out that not only were you cheating on your poor, helpless wife, but you were also preying on young innocent students and getting them pregnant?"

"Hey look. She is grown and consented to everything we did."

"True. I give you that, but you are still considered a person of authority who, from what I can tell, took advantage of the situation. So, just let me be real clear with you Mr. Passionate Professor, you're gonna do right by my daughter and my friend. Yeah, that's right – you so fucking stupid, you didn't even realize that the two women you've been screwing are family. Guess you should've kept your 'intellect' in your pants," Sherita was on a roll.

"Sir, here's your card and your receipt. I hope you enjoyed your meal," the waitress approached the table hesitantly as it did not look like a pleasant conversational exchange.

Standing up abruptly Rico, snatched his credit card off the table and crossed his satchel over his shoulders. Peering angrily into Sherita's eyes he looked as if he could kill at that very moment.

Just as he was about to speak to give Sherita a piece of his mind, Kroy walked up.

Sensing that this guy was about to attempt to disrespect his wife, Kroy needed to interject quickly.

"Is there a problem here, bruh?" Kroy asked calmly as he stood next to his wife with his shoulders squared and ready to react to whatever Rico delivered.

"Naw, ain't no problem," he responded as he sized up Kroy and then glanced at Sherita with a look of anger.

Rico turned and walked out of the restaurant without looking back. He walked briskly up the street as he searched his pocket for his cellphone. This all must be some sort of joke, right? What did she mean the two women were family? How is that possible? Once he found his phone, he called Alana.

Kroy was infuriated with Sherita. Giving her an evil look, he headed back to their table to pay the bill. Sherita followed behind him trying to explain.

"Honey, I'm sorry! I had to…."

"You had to WHAT? Sherita," Kroy said angrily. "You HAD to step to a man that you know nothing about to confront him about his life, his actions! Are you kidding me? What if he had become violent with you? THEN WHAT?"

"Kroy, I didn't think he…"

"THAT IS THE SMARTEST THING YOU'VE SAID ALL DAY…. YOU DON'T THINK!!!! This is not Atlanta! You don't know anything about this man or his capabilities. So, you don't just approach a stranger in a restaurant and attempt to play Perry Mason or some damn body because you feel like YOU'VE got something to say!"

Kroy's island accent was thick in the midst of his anger. Snatching the receipt off the table, he turned and headed for the door.

Sherita decided it best not to speak and followed her husband out of the restaurant.

After walking a couple blocks, they ended up in front of Alana's building. The main door was slightly ajar so the two headed on in without buzzing her apartment. As they reached the third floor, they could hear what sounded like arguing. Rico had come to confront Alana about his altercation with Sherita in the restaurant. Hearing the sounds of breaking glass coming from the apartment, Kroy and Sherita rushed inside the door and found Rico straddling Alana with his hands grasping her throat trying to choke her.

"ALANA!!!" Sherita screamed.

Kroy quickly charged toward Rico and proceeded to tussle with him for what felt like forever. Alana lay coughing uncontrollably on the floor as Sherita rushed to her side to help her daughter catch her breath.

"You sorry motherfucker, how dare you touch my daughter!!" Kroy was infuriated as he landed a right hook across Rico's jaw.

Struggling to maintain his footing, Kroy slipped on the throw rug just beneath his feet giving Rico the opportunity to take advantage of his shot at Kroy with all his might.

Reacting quickly to the situation, Sherita grabbed the lamp off the table next to her and hit Rico upside the head with it. He instantly fell to the floor dazed and visibly in pain. Just as she raised the lamp to whack him again, the NYPD rushed in the door. "Ma'am, drop your weapon!!" yelled the officers.

"MOM!!" Alana cried out.

Realizing she was standing over Rico with the lamp raised ready to extend a healthy blow she knew that in that moment she could kill him. Hearing Alana's voice she snapped back and became aware of her surroundings. She slowly lowered the lamp and willingly tossed it to the side. Breathing hard all she could think of was her kids and her husband and that this man was trying to hurt them. Stepping across Rico, Sherita embraced her daughter as tightly as she could. Kroy limped his way over to his family and sat on the arm of the sofa in pain.

"Oh honey, I am so sorry…." Sherita said as she kneeled down beside him to extend him some comfort.

"Mon Amore don't ever do that again," Kroy said out of breath.

"I'm sorry, baby, I promise I won't."

The police officer handcuffed Rico and sat him on the step outside the apartment door.

243

It appeared as though the neighbor across the hall had called the police when Rico first arrived because of his lewd behavior in kicking and screaming in the door for Alana to open up.

"OK, so who wants to tell us what is going on here?" The officer asked sarcastically.

"Sir, I think I can explain," Sherita said as she raised her hand asking for permission to speak.

"Mom, what are you guys doing here?" Alana asked.

"Ma'am, do you live here?"

"No, this is my daughter. She lives here."

"Then I think I need to hear from her," the officer said. "Young lady, start from the top."

CHAPTER 26

Kendra paced the floor nervously holding her phone in her hand tightly. It had been at least 30 minutes since she spoke with Sherita, and she had a strange feeling something bad had happened. She dialed Sherita's number several times and it kept going straight to voicemail. Kroy's cell was going straight to voicemail as well, which was even more strange.

Kendra was scared, she didn't know what else to do. She decided to call Tyrone.

"Hello?" Tyrone answered looking inquisitively at the phone with Kendra's name popping up.

"Hey Ty, it's me Kendra."

"Yeah, I know. What's up? Everything OK?"

"I'm not sure. I got a call from Sherita about a half hour ago and she was whispering and talking rapidly about being in a restaurant in New York and standing feet away from Rico. I think she was going to confront him."

"Who is Rico?"

"Rico! Rico, the asshole that is at the center of all of this mess with me and Alana!"

"Oh, I didn't know his name. So, how did Sher get to a restaurant with him?"

"I don't know Ty! You know Sher, she probably hired a fucking private investigator to find the dude.

My point is, it has been 30 minutes or more since I spoke with her and neither she nor Kroy are answering their phones. Ty, I think something has happened."

"Ok, just calm down. Now, Sherita is a lot of things, but all the way crazy she is not; and besides, Kroy isn't going to let her do something stupid."

"Ty, what are they doing in New York anyway?"

"Well, we decided that it was best that she go and speak with Alana face-to-face to get a better understanding of exactly what was going on with this professor and this situation she is in," he answered.

"Hold on. Let me try Sher on the other line," Tyrone picked up his house phone and dialed the number. Getting voicemail, he hung up and called Alana.

Kendra continued to pace the floor back and forth as she waited patiently on the phone for Tyrone to make a connection.

Alana sat shaking on the sofa as she explained to the police officer her relationship with Rico.

Kroy, lovingly stood over Sherita rubbing her back as he shook his head in amazement at all that had taken place. The group was distracted by Alana's ringing cellphone on the kitchen counter. Sherita got up to retrieve it. She noticed that it was Tyrone. Unable to speak with him, she handed the phone to Kroy and he answered. "Hello."

"Um, hello? Alana?" Tyrone was confused at the male voice answering his daughter's phone.

"Hey Tyrone, it's me Kroy."

"Kroy? Is everything OK? Where is Alana? Where is Sherita?" Tyrone rattled off question after question.

"Ty! What is going on?" Kendra yelled from the other phone helplessly.

"Well, yes. Everyone is fine, now," Kroy replied.

"Now? Kroy, what the hell happened?" Tyrone was anxious.

"It is a long story to tell in this moment, but Sherita confronted Rico at the restaurant, and he came to attack Alana and we made it just in time to stop his actions. Sherita and Alana are speaking with the NYPD right now giving a statement."

"WHAT? POLICE? Kroy, is my daughter, OK?"

"OH MY GOD! TYRONE WHAT IS HAPPENING? TALK TO ME!!!" Kendra screamed with fear.

"Yes, she is OK. She is a bit shaken up, but she is fine. I assure you that I am not going to let ANYTHING happen to our family," Kroy reassured Tyrone.

"Is she there? Can I speak with her?"

"Hold on a moment, let me see."

Kroy, asked the police officer if it was OK that Alana speak with her father briefly to reassure him of her safety. The officer complied and walked out into the hallway where Rico was also giving his statement.

"Daddy," Alana said with a trembling voice and tears in her eyes.

"Baby girl, are you alright?"

"Yes. I am now. Daddy, I was so scared."

"I know baby. But you're safe now. Your Mom and Kroy are there, and they aren't going to let anyone hurt you ever. I love you so much sweetie and we are going to get through this mess, I promise," Tyrone was nervous and relieved all at the same time.

As he continued his conversation with Alana, he heard a faint banging sound and realized he'd forgotten that Kendra was on the other phone.

"Alana, sweetie, hold on."

"Kendra."

"Oh My God, Ty! What the fuck is wrong with you? Why didn't you say something? I am freaking out over here!!" Kendra was livid.

"Kendra. I know. I'm sorry. Calm down, everything is OK. They are alright."

"Everything is NOT OK, I heard you say something about the police! What the hell happened, Ty?"

"It appears as though there was a scuffle involving Rico and the police are there now taking statements from Alana and Sherita. Listen, let me finish talking with them, and I will call you right back."

"Call me back? Hell No! I called you and you are going to tell me what the fuck is going on!"

"KENDRA! I will call you back," Tyrone hung up.

"Alana? Sweetie, you still there?"

"Yes Daddy. What's wrong with Aunt Kendra?"

"She's just worried about you and your mother. By the way, where is your mother?"

"She's right here. Do you want to speak with her?"

"Please," Tyrone said sarcastically.

Handing the phone to Sherita, Alana stood up and felt light-headed.

"Honey, are you alright?" Sherita asked.

"Yeah, I just need to go to the restroom. Here, Daddy wants to talk to you."

"Hey Ty."

"Sherita! What in the hell is going on up there? We didn't agree to you going to play Inspector Gadget and confront the guy."

"Tyrone, calm down! It wasn't like that. It just so happened…"

Just as Sherita was about to go into details surrounding her encounter with Rico in the restaurant, they heard a loud noise down the hall toward the bathroom. Kroy stood and rushed down the hall to find Alana passed out on the floor lying in a pool of blood. He yelled!

"OFFICER! OFFICER! Help! Call an ambulance quick!"

"Oh my God! Alana! Baby!"

"SHER! WHAT'S HAPPENING?" Tyrone yelled through the phone.

Sherita dropped the phone as she rushed to be by her daughter's side. As she knelt down beside Alana, she realized there was a puddle of blood.

"Attention 9-1-1 dispatch this is Officer Conway of the NYPD, we need an ambulance to 107 Westview Boulevard third floor apartment 825. I've got a 21-year-old African American female who has passed out and appears to be bleeding externally.

She is between 8 to 12 weeks pregnant, 5 foot 1 inches tall and approximately 130 pounds," the officer spoke into the walkie talkie on his shoulder.

"Copy that Officer Conway. We have dispatched emergency units to 107 Westview Boulevard third floor apartment 825. Paramedics should be on the scene in approximately 3 minutes."

As the officer finished up his call with the 9-1-1 dispatcher, the other officer proceeded to do CPR on Alana with Sherita yelling in tears and disbelief. Kroy stood holding his wife so that the officers could work on Alana. Within minutes, the paramedics came rushing up the steps.

Rico sat handcuffed in the back of the patrol car confused seeing the paramedics race past the car up the steps heading toward Alana's apartment.

"HEY! WHAT IS GOING ON?" he yelled through the glass.

Creating a scene, people started to gather on the sidewalk hoping to get a hint of what was happening. Many of the onlookers recognized Rico from the recent photos of him on the news. They started yelling obscenities at him in the back of the car, with a couple of the men going so far as to spit on the window that protected him from the growing mob.

"Hey! Hey! Back away from the patrol car now. That is an order," the officer yelled as he came down the stairs.

The paramedics worked feverishly to help Alana regain consciousness as they rushed her on the gurney into the back of the ambulance.

Sherita and Kroy were in tow looking desperate and afraid. Sherita hopped into the back of the ambulance with Alana, and Kroy rode in one of the patrol cars with an officer to the local hospital. Kroy realized that Tyrone was on the phone and was probably freaking out. He decided to call him to give him an update.

"Hello! Kroy! Oh My God man, what is happening? Is Alana alright?" Tyrone answered feverishly.

"Ty, no. She is not alright. Just as she handed the phone to Sher to speak with you she headed down the hall to the restroom and collapsed. Sherita is with her in the ambulance now and we are headed to the hospital," Kroy was talking extremely fast.

"What hospital? Where are they taking her?"

"Um, I'm not sure. Hold on."

"Sir, what hospital are we headed to?" Kroy asked the officer as he whisked them through the busy New York traffic.

"Sir, we are headed to Mercy General West."

"Thank you."

"Ty, we are headed to Mercy General West. I will call you as soon as we get there and give you an update."

"Kroy…. man, you make sure nothing happens to my little girl. DO YOU HEAR ME? MAKE SURE MY LITTLE GIRL IS OK!" Tyrone yelled in frustration as he pounded his fist on the countertop at the thought of being so far away and helpless.

"Ty, I promise," Kroy replied as he hung up the phone.

Tyrone was devastated and felt like he needed to be in New York. Just as he was about to book a flight Kendra called back.

"Ty, any word? What's happening?"

"Kendra, there's been an accident and they are on their way to the hospital with Alana. Apparently, she collapsed and passed out on the way to use the restroom. I don't know any more than that, but I am about to book a flight to New York."

"Oh my God! Oh my God! Tyrone, book me one, too, I am going with you! I will meet you at the airport in an hour," Kendra hung up.

The phone rang once again, and it was Josh. He'd been at work all day and had no clue as to what was going on.

"Hello."

"Hey dad. What's up? How are you today?" Josh said with excitement. Today was his first day back at work and he had a pretty good day. He missed his friends and the crazy customers at Greenbriar Mall.

"Um, son. Your sister has had an incident," Tyrone didn't feel like beating around the bush.

"What?"

"Your Mom and Kroy are in New York."

"Yeah, I know. I was calling to see if you could come pick me up from work? What's going on Dad? Is Alana OK?"

"Son, I don't know. They are on the way to the hospital now by ambulance and I am about to book a flight to New York now."

"Dad, I have to go with you! I don't need any clothes; can you just pick me up on your way to the airport?"

"I will be there in an hour, son."

Tyrone hung up and called the airlines to book 3 flights immediately.

Just as he headed to the bedroom to throw some jeans in a bag, he was confronted by Felicia. In all the hustle and bustle he hadn't even thought about her.

"So, I guess it is Team Tyrone to the rescue again, huh?" she said with her arms crossed as she leaned against the wall.

"Sweetie. It's my family," Tyrone pleaded.

"NO Ty! I'm your family! Sherita should be able to handle everything that is going on with your daughter and send you an email with any fucking updates you need! I am tired of this shit Tyrone and if you walk out that door, I swear I am leaving and I won't be coming back," Felicia's ultimatum was fierce.

Tyrone stood lifeless for what seemed like an eternity. He really did love Felicia and knew that in time they would make it past all of this, and things would balance themselves out. He looked into his wife's eyes and knew that she wanted an answer.

"Well? What's it gonna be Ty?"

"Well…take whatever you want and if need be, we can make arrangements for you to come and get the rest of your stuff. I told you time and time again, I love my ex-wife, I can't do anything about that, but I love my kids more. So, if you can't find it within yourself to understand that, then, this just wasn't meant to be."

Staring at Tyrone in disbelief, Felicia's eyes filled with water. Was he serious? She didn't know what to say. Tyrone turned to head down the hall to pack a bag.

Chapter 27

Tyrone, Kendra and Josh rushed down the hall at Mercy General West toward the information desk. They each were exhausted and worried about Alana. Having not spoken with Sherita or Kroy since earlier in the day, the three were anxious to find out what happened.

"Excuse me Miss, I am looking for my sister, Alana Coleman," Josh said politely to the lady at the desk.

"Coleman, Coleman…. ah yes, here she is. Looks like she hasn't been put in a room just yet, so you may find her still in the ER. Go down the hall, make a right at the water fountain, follow the green carpeted area to the end of the hall and the entrance to the emergency room is on the left."

"OK, thank you."

"Do you need your parking validated?"

"Ah, no ma'am. Thank you."

Without hesitation, the trio headed in the direction of the emergency room. As they rounded the corner, Tyrone spotted Sherita standing at the nurse's desk filling out paperwork.

"Sherita!"

"Oh my God, Ty! Thank God you're here," she said as she embraced her ex-husband. "Kendra, Josh I didn't expect to see you two as well," she said.

"Mom, are you serious right now, did you actually think I was going to let something happen to my sister and NOT be here if it were possible?" Josh replied as he leaned in to hug his mother.

"Yeah, Sher, girl are you trippin' or something? Did you think we weren't going to be on the next thing smoking to get here?"

"Well, I am glad you're all here, and I know Alana will be glad as well when she wakes up."

"Where is she? Is she alright?" Tyrone asked.

"Yes. She's fine now. Kroy is in the room with her I came out to finish filling out the insurance papers. Physically, she is going to be fine. She did, however, lose the baby. It seems as though the stress that she's been under the past few weeks and then hitting the floor as hard as she did when Rico attacked her all came to a head at once. The doctor indicated that even before the altercation it is a high probability that she would've miscarried anyway because her blood pressure and blood count levels were extremely low."

"Wait? Are you saying Lan was attacked?" Josh asked with concern on his face.

Looking at one another, Tyrone and Sherita realized that Josh had been out of the loop the past few days regarding the latest revelations surrounding Alana and Kendra's pregnancy saga.

Kendra was even a bit perplexed at the moment because even she didn't know the full scope of the story.

"Yes, son. Alana was attacked by the father of her unborn child.

It is a long story and before I get into details, let me finish up this paperwork. Why don't you all go on in and see her for a bit. She's been sedated but in and out of consciousness. They are supposed to be moving her to a room in the next half hour or so."

Josh and Kendra held hands as they headed toward Alana's room. Tyrone stayed with Sherita at the desk while she finished the paperwork.

"Sher, what really happened in that apartment earlier?"

"Ty it was unbelievable. I don't think I've ever come that close to killing another human being. After he rushed out the restaurant, we didn't realize he was going to head to her apartment. The thought just never crossed our mind. As we got inside the hallway to the building, all we could hear was yelling and screaming and a dog barking. It wasn't until I heard Alana's voice yelling for help that I just took off like a track runner and sprinted up three flights of stairs. Just as I got to the top, all I could see was him standing over her on the floor with one hand around her neck as if he was about to punch her with the other one. Kroy rushed past me and tackled him to the ground and started tussling with him. Man, at one point all I remember is him with his back to me as he was fighting with Kroy and I just picked up the nearest thing to me at the time which was a lamp; and if the officer hadn't yelled for me to drop my weapon, I would've killed him with one swoop. That police officer saved his life."

Staring in amazement at his ex-wife, Tyrone ran his hand across his head in disbelief. He knew that Sherita was a strong woman, but in that moment, he realized that her love for her kids and her family were unparalleled.

Maybe it was a good thing that he didn't make the trip with her. Had he walked in and seen Rico standing over his daughter, he would've reacted the exact same way.

"Wow. Well, it's over now and as fate would have it, she no longer has to deal with that creep ever again. I'm not saying that I'm glad she had a miscarriage, but things happen for a reason," Tyrone said.

"Yeah, I guess you're right. However, Kendra still has to deal with him."

"That's not our issue. She is a grown-ass woman and can handle her own mess."

The two walked to the room. Kroy stood to greet Tyrone at the door. Tyrone embraced him lovingly with a show of gratitude and appreciation.

"Kroy man, words can't express enough my thanks to you for all that you did, have done and will continue to do for my family. Our family. You are a good man, and I am glad that you are a part of Sherita and the kids' lives. Thank you, man. Thank you," Tyrone said with tears in his eyes as he and Kroy shared another embrace.

"Oh my God, Daddy, I am going to puke if the two of you start with the ugly cry," Alana joked in a low, painful voice.

"Oh, honey. It would be well worth it if we did," Tyrone laughed out loud as he made his way to his daughter's bedside and kissed her forehead.

Sherita hugged Kroy and kissed him gently on the lips and mouthed the words I love you in silence. Josh followed suit with a big hug for Kroy as well and kissed his mom on the cheek.

"Oh my God, where is the violinist with all this love in the room?" Kendra jokes.

"Shut up, Kendra," Tyrone said with a chuckle.

As the group shared a much-needed laugh with one another, they were all reminded that at the end of the day, it was all about family.

As the mood began to lighten, the nurse came in to check Alana's vital signs and let them know she'd be moving her to a room in the next 15 minutes, after the doctor came in to talk with them.

Just as the nurse finished her stats, the doctor came in the room.

"Good evening folks, I am Doctor Chu," the doctor announced after walking in the room.

Turning to Alana he smiled and said, "I am the attending doctor on duty this evening and will be going over some information with you about your condition. Now Alana, is it OK to talk with you now with your family here, or should we ask them to leave?"

"No sir. It's OK. This is my family and there isn't anything they don't already know about me."

"OK. Well, as I am sure you know by now, you did suffer a miscarriage.

Your fetus was right at about 8 weeks and two days old. This is not an uncommon occurrence in the first trimester of many pregnancies, as a number of things come into play that force a woman's body not to be able to carry a baby to full-term.

In your case, I would say that you are anemic, it appears as though you were under high levels of stress, which probably resulted in some early warning signs such as lightheadedness, headaches and fatigue, all of which you probably attributed to just being pregnant. Your blood pressure is slightly low, which is why we've decided to keep you overnight for observation and just make sure that with the loss of blood and the trauma that your body has experienced that you don't have any type of setback.

Your cervix still looks good despite the loss, which means in the future, should you decide to get pregnant again, you should be able to do so with proper observation by a physician. Do you have any questions?"

"Yes, doctor, my daughter took a pretty nasty blow to the head, could that have possibly had anything to do with the loss of the baby?" Sherita asked.

"Well, anything is possible. Again, based upon her low blood levels at the time the tests were run, it appears as though she's probably been losing a little blood for a couple of days and just didn't realize it. However, with that being said, she didn't show any signs of a concussion, but just a pretty nasty knot that should go away in a few days. So, I can't give you a definitive answer on that. I'm sorry."

"No. Thank you. I understand."

"Anything else? Alana, how do you feel?" asked the doctor.

"My head hurts, and I feel a little queasy in my stomach."

"OK. That is understandable. You will have a faint headache for the next 24-hours as a result of not only the knot on your head, but also remember right now your blood pressure is very low, so we are going to work to get that back up to normal as quickly as possible, so you'll start to feel better. I believe they are moving you to a room here shortly. I will be here all night and will check on you periodically to see how you're doing. But you need to get some rest," he insisted.

"OK. I will. Thank you, Doctor Chu."

"No problem. The nurse should be in shortly."

Sherita stood next to Alana's bed and stared at her as she reminisced a time when she was about 10 years old and had to have her tonsils removed. It was the only time Alana had ever been in the hospital overnight. Tyrone was so worried that day he slept in the chair all night holding Alana's hand. Wow, how time flies, she thought.

"Mom, I'm so sorry about all of this," Alana said looking in her mother's eyes.

"Baby, you don't have anything to be sorry for, it is a part of life."

"I feel numb about the miscarriage and guilty that I am not sad. Is that normal?"

"Sweetie, sometimes death comes as a way to show you that it is time to turn up the volume on your life. You only have just one life to live, and the choices and decisions you make in that life are the gateway to the happiness or sadness of your future. All things happen for a reason. You weren't ready for a baby and certainly not ready to be in the type of relationship you found yourself in. But there is a lesson that had to be learned and hopefully you've realized that lesson. I can't tell it to you, and neither can your Dad, all we can do at this point, Lan, is to help guide you in your decision-making process and be there in support of good, bad or indifferent."

"I love you, Mommy."

"I love you, too, sweetie."

"Dang. Just when I had come up with a name for the little tyke to call me. Hmph, guess I'll have to put 'Uncle Cool J Smooth' back in the vault," Josh joked.

Everyone in the room chuckled as they all gave a heavy sigh. Alana lovingly rolled her eyes at her brother's comment, they were each at peace in that moment.

Chapter 28

"Sabrina Harris! You've got a visitor," yelled the jail guard into the large recreation room full of female inmates.

Shocked to hear her name, Sabrina was curious as to who could be visiting her. It had been weeks since she went to court and her mom, and her cousin were working diligently to come up with enough money for her bail. As she entered the visitation area, she looked around in confusion as she didn't immediately see anyone she recognized. Finally, she spotted a very pretty, small framed, brown-skinned woman with shoulder length black hair standing near the entrance.

"Guard, I don't see anyone I recognize, are you sure they meant me?"

"Ma'am, I believe the lady standing over there is here to see you," he mentioned as he pointed in the direction of the unknown woman.

"Hello. I'm Sabrina Harris."

"Hello, Mrs. Harris I'm Kendra."

Shocked and unsure what to say, Sabrina knew instantly once she heard Kendra's voice who she was.

"Well, well, well to what do I owe the pleasure of meeting you, Kendra?" Sabrina said sarcastically as she sat down at the metal table and gestured to offer Kendra a seat.

"I was in the area and felt like I needed to see you face-to-face to clear up some things."

"Clear up some things? Like what? Explaining why you've been sleeping with my husband? How is it that you are carrying his bastard child? Please, tell me, exactly what do you intend to 'clear up'?" she said as she sat back in her seat with her arms crossed waiting for a reply.

"Look, I didn't come here to have an attitude with you. First of all, I do owe you an apology. I had no idea that Rico was married when I met him. He wasn't wearing a ring and that day at the funeral he approached me and asked me out for drinks. It wasn't an instant thing between us; it wasn't until he came to visit me in Atlanta that we became closer," Kendra explained.

"Wait? Funeral? What funeral are you talking about?"

"Last year at my cousin Harold's funeral in Virginia. I was only there for a few days spending time with my family when I met Rico. All I knew at the time was that he was a teacher in New York and that he and Harold were buddies from college."

"Harold is your cousin? That is how long ago it's been since you and Rico been kickin' it?"

Sabrina was amazed.

"Yes. But…"

"But what?"

"But there is more."

"More?"

"When you were calling me, you thought you were contacting Alana?"

"Yeah, supposedly he was messing around with one of his students at the university. I didn't realize he was doing a balancing act among many women."

"Yeah, well. Neither of us did. However, you are right. He was involved with Alana as well."

"How do you know that?"

"Alana is my," Kendra suddenly paused mid-sentence.

In shock, Sabrina sat up in her chair.

"Get the fuck out-of-here! Are you shittin' me right now?"

She'd been trying for a while to put two-and-two together since her phone conversation with Kendra. Seeing as how she never could get a straight answer from Rico's lying ass.

"No, I'm not," Kendra said.

"Umph, umph, umph only Rico's dumb-ass would manage to be fucking around with two women who were related and not have a clue."

"Right. He only just found out recently himself."

"Yeah? How'd he handle that information?"

"Well, something else you don't know is that Alana was pregnant as well."

"Come again?"

"She was carrying Rico's baby also. But…"

"Wait a minute. You mean to tell me that both y'all bitches is pregnant by my fucking husband? My husband?" she said yelling as she stood up.

"HARRIS! SIT DOWN!" the guard yelled in a warning tone.

Breathing heavy and looking around with tears streaming down her face, Sabrina was infuriated at this information. She cautiously sat back down as she aggressively wiped the tears from her face with the back of her hands. Kendra felt sorry for Sabrina. She could see the betrayal in her eyes and the hurt she was feeling.

"You said she was pregnant?"

"Yeah. She lost the baby yesterday."

"How?" Sabrina asked with an unexpected look of concern on her face.

"She had a miscarriage after Rico attacked her."

"He did what? Attacked her? Is she OK?" She asked rapidly one question after the other.

"Yeah. She is fine. But Rico is in county lockup for simple battery charges."

"I hope his ass rots in hell."

"Look, I felt obligated to come and see you and personally say I'm sorry for the pain I have caused you. Had I known that Rico was married, he would have automatically been off limits to me. Trust me when I tell you, I grapple everyday with the fact that I am going to raise a baby who one day I will have to tell them who their father is and how I met him. I am not proud of that. Now I can't do anything about how you handle things with Rico, but I felt like if you knew the truth that it would help you move on in some small way."

Overwhelmed with this information and Kendra's kindness, Sabrina sat there, staring off into the distance. After a long pause, she sat up and looked Kendra straight in the eye.

With her head held high and a sense of pride, she said….

"Thank you. I appreciate you being woman enough to come here. Most bitches, I mean, women wouldn't care about how the wife feels in this situation."

The two women sat staring at one another in silence for a few seconds.

"So, how far along are you?" Sabrina asked, trying to make small talk.

"4 months."

"Well, I wish you luck. Looking at you, I can see what attracted Rico to you. You're beautiful."

"Thank you. So are you."

"Yeah, well…orange really isn't my best color," she joked.

As the two laughed for a brief moment, it wasn't long before the guard told them that their time was up.

"Hey. You take care of yourself in there, you hear me?" said Kendra as she reached across the table and touched Sabrina's hand.

"I will do my best."

Kendra stood and watched as they escorted Sabrina back through the steel set of double doors.   She was saddened at all that had taken place and felt like there must be something she could do to help Sabrina. Before heading out of the police station, she stopped by the information desk to ask a quick question.

"Excuse me, I'd like release information for Mrs. Sabrina Harris please."

"Harris. Yeah, she's been in here for a minute; seems as though her family is having a difficult time coming up with the rest of her bail money."

"Really? How much more do they owe?"

"Looks like $5,000.00."

"How long after it's paid will she be released? And then what happens?"

"Well, once the amount is paid in full, her lawyer will be notified, and she will be given a court date to appear to answer the charges within 30 to 45 days. She could be out within 24 – 48 hours depending on how backed up they are in release processing."

Kendra stood with an inquisitive look on her face as she tapped her fingers on the counter.

Looking at her watch, she knew she needed to head back to the hospital, so she didn't miss the flight with the family.

"Ma'am is there anything else?" the officer asked Kendra.

"Ummm, yeah. Do you take American Express?"

Chapter 29

Bella made it to the hospital just in time to see Alana before her release.

Alana decided to finish up the semester by taking online classes at home in Atlanta. She had been through so much emotionally she realized she really missed her family and needed to be around them to help move past this whole ordeal with Rico.

Knock, knock, knock....

"Someone told me there was a princess about to leave the castle and I just had to come and see for myself," Bella joked as she poked her head inside the door to Alana's room.

"BELLA!" Alana shrieked at the sight of her best friend.

The two embraced with tears in their eyes.

"Oh my God, Bella, I have missed you. Are you alright?"

"Am I alright? Girl, seeing as how I am here visiting you in the hospital, I think I should be the one asking the questions," Bella replied.

"Yeah, yeah, I am fine. I am much better now that all of this mess is over and soon to be behind me."

"I bet. Wow. The whole family came to New York, I see."

"Yeah. Well, you know my mom. That's my crazy brother Josh in the corner and… that's my dad and my stepdad. The only other person is my Aunt Kendra who said she was going downstairs to get something to eat."

"Ty, where is Kendra? She's been gone for quite some time. You don't think something has happened to her, do you?" Sherita asked, suddenly realizing that Kendra had been gone for a good while.

"I don't know, but we better find her. She still owes me money for her flight here!" he said with a chuckle.

"Dad!" Alana said laughing.

"I know right," Josh chimed in.

"What you talking about knucklehead? You owe me, too!"

"But Dad, it was a family emergency," Josh explained.

"Umm hmm. It's gonna be an emergency!"

"Mom?"

"Sorry son, I can't help you. I got a plane ticket back."

"Kroy?"

"Looks like you're in a fix my man," Kroy said smiling.

"Dang. So, ah Bella…do you need a roommate?"

The group erupted with laughter at the joyful exchange in the room.

Alana felt good having all of her family around her as she smiled lovingly at each person there.

This experience had taught her to make wiser decisions going forward. Although she knew she wasn't ready to be a mother, she was a bit melancholy at the circumstances surrounding her pregnancy.

The last thing she ever wanted to do was hurt her family. Her mom, dad and brother meant the world to her, and she knew no matter what, they would always have her back. Taking some time away from New York would do her some good. It would help her put some things back into the right perspective.

Chapter 30

Five months later…

Standing in the mirror, wrapping her hair up before bed, Sherita hums a happy tune when her cellphone started ringing. She glances at the time - 10 p.m.

"Hello."

"Sher! I think it's time. The baby is coming!"

"Really! OK, I am on my way! Just breathe, Kendra. Breathe!"

Sherita made it to Kendra's house in what seemed like 10 minutes flat. Seeing her friend in pain, she rushed to help her get in the car and head to Northside Hospital.

"Hurry, Sher! It hurts!" Kendra screamed.

"OK! OK! Hang in there honey, you're doing great."

Sherita pulled up to the expecting mother's door of the emergency room and helped Kendra out of the car. Nurses were waiting at the curb with a wheelchair to escort her to the birthing room.

Once inside, Kendra was checked by the doctor.

"Well, Kendra, looks like you're going to have a baby, but..." the doctor said as Kendra cut him off.

"But? What do you mean but?"

"But not right now. You are not even dilating."

"What do you mean, I'm not dilating? That is impossible! I am in pain!"

"It's probably just gas or Braxton Hicks contractions. So, back home you go."

"Home?"

"Yeah, home."

As the orderly brought the wheelchair around, Kendra was visibly disappointed at the news that she was going home without a baby. Sherita dropped Kendra off and offered to stay with her to keep her company, but Kendra insisted she go home and get some sleep. The two hugged and Sherita left and headed home. Exhausted, she managed to change clothes and climb into bed.

In a deep dream where she was surrounded by water, Sherita felt herself gasping for air when the sound of the ringing phone snapped her out of her sleep.

2:00 a.m.

"Hello?" Sherita answered half asleep.

"Sher! I think this is it. The baby is coming!" Kendra whispered loudly.

"Really Kendra? OK, I am on my way."

Sherita rolled out of bed and struggled to put on some sweatpants and a shirt. She grabbed her keys and her wallet off the nightstand

and headed out the door. Following the same routine, she and Kendra headed toward Northside Hospital. Greeted by a new set of nurses the two went through the motions again with the wheelchair escort. Once inside, Kendra is checked by the doctor.

"Well Kendra, looks like you're going to have a baby, but…"

"But what?" Kendra said sternly as she continued panting like a dog.

"But not right now. You've only dilated 2 centimeters since we last saw you and that isn't even enough to induce labor at this point. You could be at this stage for hours or even days."

"Days? Oh, hell no! This baby is coming out today!" Kendra was furious.

"Kendra, just calm down," Sherita said.

"Calm down! I've been pregnant for what feels like a year and you're telling me to calm down. I can't go days, Sher! I promise you; I can't do it!"

"Kendra. It's gonna be fine. Now come on, let me take you home."

In tears and cursing under her breath, Kendra was once again wheeled to the car. The two rode in silence, as they commenced the same routine as before. Sherita offered to stay but was glad when Kendra sent her home. At this point, she just wanted a couple of hours of sleep in her own bed.

As she dozed off, it felt like she had just fallen asleep.

5:00am – Sherita is annoyed as she glares at the ringing phone on the nightstand.

"Kendra?"

"Sherita, I promise you this is it. My water just broke."

"Are you sure your water broke Kendra or did you pee on yourself again?" Sherita was aggravated and sleepy.

"What? No, I didn't pee on myself. I'm serious, Sher. I'm in labor!" she said, screaming in between the contractions.

"How far apart are the contractions?"

"About… 4 minutes," she replied between breathing noises.

"4 minutes? Oh shit! I'm on my way."

Sherita flew down the highway toward Northside Hospital, this time with Kendra in the passenger seat sweating, panting and screaming for dear life. She was nervous and excited at the same time for her friend. She knew that Kendra was going

to be a good Mommy and couldn't wait to meet her new godchild. Kendra decided early on that she didn't want to know the sex of the baby and wanted it to be a surprise. Sherita didn't really care what it was as long as it was healthy.

Back to the routine in front of the hospital, a new set of nurses greeted the two best-friends on the curb with a wheelchair. Panting heavily and holding her stomach, somehow the two of them both knew that this was it. The hospital staff rushed Kendra into the birthing room and prepped Sherita for the delivery.

Wow, who would've thought all those years ago in eighth grade that these two women would still be sharing one another's joys in life. Kendra and Sherita had been through so much together that neither of them could ever imagine a time without the other.

"SHER!"

"I'm right here, sweetie. Just breathe, everything is going good. You are doing a great job."

"OK Kendra. This is it. This is the day you get to meet your baby," the doctor said.

"OH! GET IT OUT!" she yelled.

"OK, so here is what I need you to do. When I count to three, I want you to push. Not until I say three, understood?"

"YES!"

"Here sweetie, grab my hand tight," Sherita encouraged.

"OK Kendra, here we go. One! Two! Three....push, push, push, push, push," the doctor encouraged.

"You're doing great, honey. Hang in there."

"OK, last one. On three, I need you to push as hard as you can. I already see the baby's head, so one more good push should do. You ready?"

"Yeah," she said out of breath.

"All right, one! Two! Three. PUSH KENDRA YOU CAN DO IT!"

The room suddenly erupted into echoing baby cries. Loud and strong telling the world a new arrival was in the midst.

"It's a BOY KENDRA! It's a BOY!" Sherita yelled, jumping up and down clapping with tears of joy in her eyes.

The nurses quickly wiped him off and laid him on Kendra's chest, calming his wailing cries almost instantly. Sherita stood over her friend with a loving gaze as she met her bouncing baby boy for the first time.

"Look, Sher, it's a boy," she said with tears.

"I know a beautiful baby boy and I am so proud of you girl; you did good. Real good."

"Yeah, he's perfect, huh?"

"Well, what else would you expect? He's got a perfect Mommy."

"I hope so."

"So, what are we going to call this handsome little fellow?"

"Sabin Alexander Williams."

"Wow. I like it," Sherita confirmed with a smile.

"Well, Mom, your little bundle of joy was born at exactly 6:02 a.m. weighing in at 7 pounds 2 ounces and 19 inches long. Welcome to parenthood," the doctor said.

Once the doctor finished up his announcement, the nurses clapped and cheered for Kendra and her new journey into motherhood. She was thrilled to meet her new baby boy and instantly forgot all about what had gone on prior to his arrival. Kendra knew early on that if she didn't have this baby, she would probably never have kids. Her decision to be a single parent was a tough one, but she was reminded that she was surrounded by family. Sherita and her family were Kendra's family, and her baby would have so much love and joy in his life, that he wouldn't miss a thing.

As Sherita busied herself taking photos and texting the announcement of her newborn nephew, Kendra's thoughts drifted for a second to Sabrina. She hadn't heard from her since she paid the remaining balance on her bail to help get her out of jail. Sabrina called once in the days that followed but didn't leave a message. Kendra knew that she was thankful. She hoped that her life was getting back on track and that soon she would find the happiness she deserved.

It's funny how life takes you on a rollercoaster of challenges, but fate wins in the end.

Tracye D. Bryant

Acknowledgments

A heartfelt thank you goes out to all my family and friends who continue to support me and my writing. Trust me, this journey would not be possible without each of you pushing and praying for me daily and for that I am truly grateful. Again, thank you.

CPSIA information can be obtained
at www.ICGtesting.com
Printed in the USA
LVHW052150150422
716361LV00007B/21

9 780997 694642